The professional

'It's a take-out mission. Cuba. The agent is there now, waiting ... You are to save her if possible ... But if absolutely necessary you are also authorized to waste her.'

The Firm's orders, succinct and devastating, force Guerin into the deadliest assignment of his long and experienced career. Lonely, withdrawn, deprived of his identity by the demands of a ruthless organization, Guerin is beginning to loose his cool, to blow his cover. The catalyst to this dangerous mood is Julia Fernandez, beautiful, arrogant, and an enigma.

With extraordinary realism and chilling accuracy James David Buchanan, in his first novel, has portrayed the spy's shadow-world of discipline, duplicity and extreme danger.

JAMES DAVID BUCHANAN

The professional

Constable London

First published 1972
by Constable & Company Ltd
10 Orange Street
London WC2H 7EG

Set in Linotype Pilgrim

Printed in Great Britain by
Northumberland Press Limited, Gateshead

'The soul of the spy is somehow the model of us all'
                                        Jacques Barzun

PROLOGUE

By noon an awesome heat fell with steady weight upon the paving stones of Avenida Monserrate, causing whatever residue remained from the morning rain to sizzle away. Julia moved in tempo with her surroundings, swinging her large handbag with calculated casualness even though she was certain that the beating of her heart must be visible to any passerby. Dark glasses hid her eyes although the streets had been so emptied of life there was scarcely anyone around to shield them from. As it was, they reduced her problems by one in keeping out the worst of the glare, and the rest was simply anxiety. Wary, instinctive, she glided liquidly on through a ghost city of sun-bleached walls and the shadows of her own fears which danced against them, moving with her. In a few hours it would be over. The worst of it.

The rain had brought out aggressive numbers of insects, as unusual as the heat even in midsummer. Julia thought of them as the buzzing of the sun and hardly made any gesture to drive them away. She had read in *Hoy* how in China they had marshalled the resources of the entire nation, including school children, to virtually eliminate flies, and caught herself wishing idly they would begin that here. Ridiculous, she would not be around to benefit from it.

A *campesino*, as dark as herself, with a freshly scrubbed face and tattered but clean clothes, stopped to admire her as she went by. 'Chi-chi-chi-chi ...' Ordinarily she would not have minded, but now it first frightened and then infuriated her; she felt like yelling at him. In her mind

7

she called him a goat and denounced the revolution that had made him its child, but all this was only fantasy. Julia was still young, loved life, she wanted to survive. She broke the rhythm of concern by wondering how that peasant would react if he knew who she was and where she was going—how he would run! Like all the peasants in history, up until now anyway, he would not want to get involved. She quickly forgot about him.

By the time she reached the Church of the Angel it was possible to hear the chanting crowds on the Prado in front of the Capitol: 'Feeeedel ... Feeeedel ... Feeeedel ...' Politics aside, it sounded almost festive enough to make her wish she could be there to share in the excitement. She could see how even the speeches, running on as they did for hours, were bearable if shared with enough of those who had existed for generations in a world where no one of power or substance ever bothered to speak directly to you about anything. Again it was necessary to shift emotions; she could not, she realized, allow herself to think this way now that she had come so far. Any vacillation at all, any failure to apply the maximum resolve, to act boldly, could put her against the wall in the moat of the Cabana. And no one on the tribunal would care in the least about the complex of contradictory feelings and threats she would say had caused her to act in the way that she had.

Julia did not deny the firing wall on philosophical grounds, she recognized that the state must be defended according to the code of revolutions, but she had a special objection to their shooting women there—men had always killed each other that way since the invention of gunpowder and before that with arrows, and their bodies were constructed for giving and receiving punishment, but was there not something obscene about the ritualistic puncturing of breasts and wombs by small angry bees of lead? She had often considered lately whether you wore

8

things like brassières and girdles and high heels or whether there was not some decently neuter garment for the occasion.

It was only a couple of more blocks to the Ministry. Ridiculously, she found herself wondering if she had applied sufficient cologne to compensate for the inordinate heat. A little boy on his way to the Prado whistled at her and she found the courage to smile. Of course, all women were beautiful here.

At Calle Chacon she ran into her first barricade; it was manned by a *miliciana* carrying a machine pistol and wearing, Julia noted, high heels. What a pretty little thing, she thought, and yet the bullets from that single clip would tear her apart should that delicate, long-nailed finger apply a few ounces of pressure in anger or panic. Julia showed her papers.

'Aaaaaiee, what's wrong with you, girl? You don't mean you're going to work today?'

'For a few hours, why not?' Julia replied, eyeing the girl critically. 'Do you suppose they celebrated national holidays in the Sierra Maestra?'

The girl waved her through with a sour face. 'I wouldn't know,' she answered at the last moment, 'I was only a child at the time.'

By the time she reached the steps of the Ministry, the chanting had been replaced by periodic roars, great bright columns of sound that battered at the sensibilities and made a detached person feel small and defenceless. These punctuated the single reverberating male voice that aimed through a sound system which effectively garbled its meaning beyond a block or two. It was not even possible to identify the speaker with certainty, although she guessed it was Dorticos. She thought ruefully that the sound equipment, like everything else mechanical in the country, was probably in need of parts or servicing ... 'ruefully' because she would herself have to count on the dependability

9

of mechanical means to effect her escape from Havana, and eventually from the island itself. She was worried about Renaldo; that old taxicab of his, a 1949 Chevrolet, was notoriously unpredictable, yet it was the only way she had of making her rendez-vous at the Chinese cemetery, for there were no buses and few, if any, cabs running in Cuba on the 26th of July.

The guard at the main entrance to the building was a boy in baggy fatigues who had often flirted with her in the past, and had received notable encouragement for his effort these last two weeks.

There was no trouble about going in and yet Julia paused on the steps. This would be the last moment she would have to look at Havana unencumbered by problems of immediate survival. Deserted in the punishing glare of the sun, rather shabby and careworn from the struggle of the last few years, it was still the pastel city she loved best of all the places she had been, and the only one where she had been happy even for a little while. From somewhere came the rich acidulous smell of a lemon tree. Then, out of the corner of her eye, she saw that the guard was studying her curiously. She turned and flashed him a smile she hoped would be reassuring, or hopefully even devastating, as she went inside.

The Ministry had been built in the time of Machado the Butcher and suffered the best and the worst of what happens to public buildings in the tropics. Lately, attempts had been made to give it a modern and functional appearance on the outside, but none of that had affected its dank interior. The emptiness of the halls exaggerated the sound of her heels on the tile floor and she looked down involuntarily, only to find herself admiring the delicate symmetry of the inlays for the first and last time. She went straight to her desk, got out a variety of papers and turned on the asthmatic overhead fan just as if she intended to spend the day there. Then she waited.

Half an hour went by in an agony of nerves while she tried to look busy lest someone happen by or there was some means of surveillance she did not know about. When she had been given the assignment she had baulked at the timetable which forced her to be on the scene so early, but it had been explained that the very fact of the 26th of July celebration, while it provided an excellent cover, made it necessary to broaden options as much as possible, allowing for extraordinary security precautions on the streets, unexpected military manoeuvres, the capriciousness of crowds and so on. Now that she was here there was nothing to do but to wait out the one dangerous guard, a G-2 man, who went around on a security check approximately at three, and her ride out which was due at three-thirty.

There were several things about the assignment that seriously troubled Julia—but primarily its simplicity. She had been given a key to Major Espinoza's office and another for the particular file, they were in the compartment in her purse where she would put the documents when she got them out, but obviously this meant that there was someone else from her own component working in the Ministry, yet she had never been told this and indeed her controller had still refused to confirm it even as he handed over the keys. Whoever it was, why had *they* not simply walked in and removed the papers?

Julia had not been told what they contained, but only a means of identifying them by colour, location and file number. They would be in a green envelope and she had been given strict instructions not to open it. Well, she had reassured the controller, why should she care about that part of it when most of the things she had handed on were unknown quantities to her; she was not a professional agent and she assumed it was that way all over the world. He had heard her out and then methodically repeated the warning not to examine the papers under any circumstance.

Someone went down the hall and Julia drew in her breath in fear that they would come in seeking conversation, although she could not imagine any of the regular employees of the Ministry coming in today. She soon identified them as a man's footsteps and glanced at the wall clock; it was the three o'clock security round. They came closer and she found herself wishing she had not left the door of her office open, even though it had been done specifically so she would not look surreptitious. Now, as the moment approached, she was no longer sure she could control herself in a confrontation of any kind. If the man saw her, however, he gave no sign and continued on down the hall. Julia began to breathe evenly again as the footsteps receded. It was time for her move.

She took her purse and headed in the direction of the women's lavatory, but midway ducked into the stairwell and hurried to the floor above. If she was caught here there was no logical excuse possible. And yet she ran right into a girl named Maria a few doors from Major Espinoza's office, exchanged nods and went on. Perhaps the girl did not know her well enough to realize that she had no business being there. The key, a reproduction, worked stiffly in the lock, giving her a bad moment, but it worked in the end. She disengaged the alarm system on the inner door that led to the files as she had been instructed and found the envelope almost immediately. She knew she should have gone back to her own office and straightened it out, if only to delay suspicion, and then left routinely, but she could not trust herself to carry it off.

Out and down the hall, the clacking of her heels no longer a cause for nostalgia but echoing through the empty building like gun shots. Would Renaldo be waiting? There were a dozen places where he could have run into a roadblock and been commandeered for some petty reason or other. She could try it on foot; it would take hours but it was unlikely anyone would find anything amiss until she failed to show up for work the next morning. Still, she would miss her rendezvous at the Chinese cemetery and it was not easy to get into the countryside these days. Trapped in Havana, they would run her down within a week. She went through the main entrance into the superheated air outside and it made her slightly faint, wound as tight as she was. When the blood came back, she realized Renaldo was not there. 'Oh, God!' she murmured aloud, clutching the purse to her until the knuckles whitened and her hands hurt from the effort. Next, she noticed that the guard was not there either; he was down the street, his carbine trailing in the dust while he strained to get a glimpse of the military parade which was part of the festivities. That sight prevented Julia's going to pieces.

She began to laugh in quick little spasms at the thought of one of the most important buildings in Havana, a key centre in the defence of the Revolution, being left in the hands of a small boy who would rather watch a parade. History was either totally gratuitous or it had a very distinct sense of humour when it chose a tiny band of excitable romantics to rock the Western World. She was glancing again at her watch when Renaldo came around the corner on two of his threadbare tyres and lurched to a stop at the kerb directly in front of her. Julia could not help herself, she rushed down the steps wildly, and with a face suddenly as open and gay as though she were going to a lover.

Across the street in a bare second-floor room of an apartment house requisitioned from a professional gambler, Captain Guido Cespedes of the G-2 Bureau put down his powerful glasses and watched Julia climb into the cab with satisfaction. He had no idea at this point how they

13

would get her out of the country but it was a reasonable assumption that, once clear of Havana, she would make it. He could only wait.

Julia, for her part, was still smiling to herself as Renaldo drove in disgruntled silence away from the centre of the city. She had had to warn him once to slow down lest he attract attention, and he was pouting. One of the reasons he hated the Revolution was the freedom it had given to women, and here he was suffering indignities in the service of the counter-revolution at the hands of a bitch half his age. Was there nowhere left in the world where a man was still a man? Julia was unaware of his anger and would have been indifferent to it in any event —she was lost in the reading of the papers she had stolen.

1

The Firm would wonder why he had taken a third-rate motel. They wondered about everything. Guerin was not quite sure himself, although he had known on sight that it would not have telephones in the rooms and that thought had cheered him considerably. Still, they had tracked him down, probably through the State Police, who would note the licence and report it back to Washington but would not deliver any messages themselves unless forced to. State and local officials reacted that way to the Firm generally. They were afraid of it.

He had been lying on his back, staring at the soiled ceiling, smoking a small cigar and drinking the last of a six-pack of beer he had bought at a little general store down by the lake, thinking of nothing more complicated than how much he disliked the beer in the Middle West now and how good it had tasted when he was growing up. The beer most likely had not changed. The air conditioning was only half alive and he had decided sleep was probably the best bargain he could make; with effort he got up and was looking around for the nembutal when the manager knocked. Guerin answered by opening the door a crack and asking what he wanted—it was simply habit and training that caused him to keep his face out of the light.

The manager, a sleepy-looking, dyspeptic man half in and half out of his clothes had told him : 'Your company's calling you on the telephone in the office. Said it was important,' he added, in a tone that said plainly he doubted it, himself.

Guerin apologized and promised he would hurry along.

'I got to stay up till you do,' the manager said, going away.

Guerin cursed under his breath, but it was the Firm he was angry at. They had promised him five days with his children—five days that year, he reminded himself—and there were two to go and up to now he had scarcely seen them. The court had prescribed painfully brief and precise visiting hours. That was because he had not contested the divorce, a decision he now regretted but the only one the Firm had been willing to accept at the time; in fact, it was basic policy with them and would be no different now if he were stubborn or foolish enough to open things up again. He was slightly off balance on his way down to the manager's office, the result of the two tranquillizers he had taken earlier mixing with the beer, he imagined.

'Hello, Stephen?' came the voice on the phone.

'Yes.'

'It's Charlie Ames—how are you?'

'Okay. What do you want?' Guerin was surprised at his own abruptness, but tonight the whole charade just seemed to be too much for him. He was good on voices and this was no one he had ever met or even spoken to before.

The voice steeled-up slightly. 'Listen, we've got kind of a crisis here with the Leary account and the old man wondered if you couldn't come back and help us out. *Toute suite*,' he finished, and Guerin wondered where the hell they were recruiting these days.

He looked up at the manager but the man's back was to him. He had turned on the television set in the lobby as some sort of gesture, making it hard to hear, and unwittingly encouraging Guerin by his stupid indifference to greater heights of insubordination.

'Look,' he argued, 'I was specifically promised five days with my kids. It's goddamned important to me. McNeely can get eight thousand guys for whatever the hell needs doing.'

'Probably he can, but he asked us to contact you. Can you leave tonight?'

'No, I can't. I've been ...' He didn't know why he hesitated but suddenly it sounded ridiculous. '... I went to a circus today and I'm dead. It's a five-six hundred mile drive, for Christ's sake.'

The voice on the phone was by now flat and frankly disapproving. The motel manager was watching an ancient horror movie, and Guerin felt an urgent desire to crack him over his expanse of bald head, or at least to tell him to shut the damn thing down so he could hear, but they were not like that in the Firm, they were never rude, they never drew attention to themselves under any circumstances. But with the voice on the phone it was different— he was feeling raw about the kids.

'I can authorize a plane. Drive out to Selfridge Field, that's in Mt Clemens, primarily National Guard, but—'

'I *know* where it is, I grew up here,' Guerin cut in. It was funny, he thought, the way these types started out with all the cover business and ended up, if they got the least resistance, laying it on the line. He was almost disarmed by it. Reasonably, what was there worth disguising in their conversation anyway, and who tapped the lines in obscure Michigan motels? None of the Hostiles he could think of had the time, the personnel, or would consider him, out of hand, important enough to devote a lifetime to. The only thing he cared about now was Nancy and Jack, and the pain of his tenuous, fading relationship with them.

'I'll start driving in the morning.'

The voice hesitated. 'All right. I can authorize that. But hurry along, won't you.'

'Hurry along, won't you,' Guerin muttered to himself as he put down the phone. The Eastern school boys, the ones, anyway, who carved out safe careers in Projections or Communications or Analysis, always seemed to become more English the longer they were with the Firm. He thanked the manager, who grunted in return, and went outside to breathe.

It was a warm, redolent night, the kind he had loved since he was a child here in the lee of the Great Lakes. Insects sounding and stars all around unencumbered—the red glow of Detroit, an ugly city but beautiful in reflection, was from twenty miles away. He stood still for a long time and wondered if the children were aware of things like this. Did they, Jack at least, own a telescope as he had as a boy? Did they lie on the grass at night and look up at the sky, or rise early to dig worms after a rain or know the places in Bloomfield Hills within easy pedalling distance where a boy could eat a bag lunch out of sight deep in a sumac thicket? He did not really know any children but he had the uneasy feeling that they no longer found things like crayfish and bluegills terribly exciting, even in the Middle West. These were things he should know, would have known had his life been different. He lit up the stub of the cigar and let the smoke out slowly. He could send them a telescope, one for each perhaps. It would be as if from a stranger, but that was all he could do. He went back to his room to look for the nembutal, which he had hidden from himself.

In the morning, though he had slept less than six hours, he felt a little better. There was no particular reason why he should, other than the clear-eyed inevitability dawn gives to the unhappiest choices. His resolution grew as he prepared to check out of the motel, and by the time he got on the road, he had decided that this morning would be the last occasion on which he would see the children. They had another father now and seemed to like him, indeed hardly rose above politeness with Guerin—anything less than a total break would be selfish on his part. And there was certainly nothing else left to draw him back to this part of the country at his age; school friends had died, moved away or changed, some of them beyond recognition. If he did run into someone he knew there were not five truly honest words he could put one after another. Even his name was a lie of four years' standing and so well integrated he felt uncomfortable and somehow guilty when confronted with the one his dead parents had given him. It might well be that only sophomores quoted Wolfe, but he could think of no better way to vector it for himself than the reminder that 'you can't go home again'.

He took the long way around the lake in order to sort things out. Besides, it was only nine o'clock and Janice was a late riser; he did not want an argument if he could help it, not when he needed a favour. Suddenly hungry, he looked around for somewhere to eat breakfast, but he had waited too long, there was nothing but residential elegance as far as the eye could roam. Janice had made a wise choice, as Janice would.

He slipped his hard-used Mustang onto the shoulder where the road closely skirted the lake, the left two wheels inches from the water. Laying his head back, he massaged his temples gently with his fingertips ... The Firm. Before he walked in and said goodbye to his own children for the last time he ought to say it aloud to himself about the Firm. Like many of its people, Guerin had entered it when he was young, without hesitation and without even giving it a great deal of serious thought, although of course they did a lot of evaluation on their side. That was part of it, the gratification in being accepted by a great severe institution which laboured long and then took only a miniscule percentage of those it considered; it was irresistible, one felt as though chosen by some mysterious order in possession of the fundamental truths of his society. And especially had the professionalism attracted him, the sense of life-style; perhaps only in medicine or law would you find the devotion and concern given that particular idea more conspicuous. In a world without standards or meaning a man is what he does by default. Of course, he reminded himself, he had never heard of the 'Element' or the 'Bourse' before entering the Firm, and probably would not have believed in them if he had.

The sudden appearance of the patrolman at the window gave him a start and considerably bruised his pride. As he turned to confront the vacant, dry-boned face a few inches from his own, he thought another surprise like this and it might be well worth considering getting out of 'clandestine'. 'Motivational exhaustion', they called it at the Firm, the lessening of commitment on the part of an agent as a result of impingements on his personal and family life. If the Firm was what he was and what he did, there were no excuses for not being good at it.

'Let's see your licence,' the cop demanded in a rusty voice full of insecure authority.

Guerin handed it over, noting that the man kept one hand close to his holster, a gesture he felt unwarranted somehow at nine in the morning. But of course it was his ageing modest car in this wealthy neighbourhood.

'Washington, DC, huh. What are you doing out here?'

'Visiting my children. My wife and I are divorced.'

'They live around here, do they?'

Guerin nodded coolly—he had learned a long time ago that there were certain kinds of petty functionaries with whom it was dangerous to be polite or deferential.

'So where do they live?'

'Whitcomb. Across the lake there.' He pointed vaguely. At the same time he was worrying; if you were FBI or Secret Service it was one thing with small-town types like this, but for the Firm it sometimes meant annoyance ...

you never knew. Now he had given the man his cover and across the lake they knew him by his real name. He hoped it would not go that far.

The officer glanced at the opposite shore and then back at Guerin, studying him closely. 'What do you do there?'

'In Washington? I'm a statistician for the Department of Agriculture.'

'How come you were pulled over here? You drinking or anything?' The man actually sniffed. 'Taking any pills?'

Guerin sighed in spite of himself. 'Just a little nostalgic, officer, and also I didn't want to get there while they were still eating breakfast.'

The cop looked easier. 'Okay,' he drawled, 'but you can't just sit here, it makes the residents nervous. They called in on you.'

'Yes, well, since my children are residents, I'm pleased to find it's as secure as it apparently is around here.'

He got an ambiguous look for that, the cop was not sure whether or not he was making fun of him, but he gave it up finally and went back to his car. Guerin pulled out and noticed the police car following him part of the way, but he was indifferent now.

The Whitcomb home, a large white Colonial affair, shared an approach road with the adjacent country club. Guerin could see it through the stands of oak and poplar from a long way off. Janice had remarried with the same hard-headed practicality she showed in everything else; only with Guerin did she display more emotion than logic. He had never blamed her for the way she felt about the Firm, only a certain kind of woman could live like that. And not hating her, he wondered why she had to hate him.

The Negro maid who answered the door seemed a little disconcerted at the sight of him.

'Good morning, Alma. I'd like to see Mrs Whitcomb.'

She let him in as far as the vestibule and went to summon her mistress. When Janice entered, and it was always an entrance, a sweeping in, it was the first time Guerin had really seen her in the three days he had been there; she had made a point of not being present, sending the children down with the maid or having him escorted up to them, though a couple of times he had caught a glimpse of her going down the hall or tearing out of her driveway in an open car. She stopped and stared at him in an appraising, wide-eyed way that he well remembered from some of their best and worst moments. She was wearing a brightly flowered peignoir and had a red ribbon in her long ashen hair. Janice was thirty-six but this was early morning and her beauty was both apparent and painful. Guerin found it difficult to speak.

'What do you want, Stephen?'

'I wanted to see the children ... to say goodbye. I'm leaving ... called back.'

'You know this isn't the time, it's very strictly set down—'

'—I'm going away today—'

'—If you want them with you all day then you are entitled to have them come visit you two weeks out of every year.'

The muscles in his face tightened. She was getting to him after only a few words had been exchanged, and he hated himself for it. 'You know I can't. For God's sake, don't be cute.'

'You can see the children at one, after they've had their lunch.'

'I'll be gone.'

'Your problems are no longer my problems, Stephen.' She turned away and he grabbed her arm. She jerked it free and turned back to him, the near-contemptuous serenity gone from her eyes.

'I'll call Mike. He hasn't gone to work yet.'

'Your husband's a nice guy—leave him out of this. What are we going to do, Indian wrestle?'

'Mike can take care of himself.'

'This is juvenile, for Christ's sake, Janice. I just want to see my children. That's not so much to ask, is it? Our war's over years ago.'

'They're in summer school. They get home at one.'

She was telling the truth—he had forgotten.

'Now get out.'

Guerin accepted it and went away from her. 'You miserable bitch,' he said in the going, but more for himself than in any hope of hurting her.

'Someday, Stephen—if I can—I'll ruin you with the Firm. Then we'll be quits.'

He heard the door slam behind him but he had no way of knowing who was there to do it, Janice or the maid, or even poor Mike Whitcomb. Suddenly he had a cosmic vision of his ex-wife working with one of the Hostile organizations, say the Chinese, to destroy him; a wealthy, spoiled, middle-aged housewife from the Middle West feeding plans and profiles to the computors of a red Fu Manchu, and that amused him. Gliding away down that long driveway he laughed right out loud. He felt freer, sad about the kids, lonely, but free. Time to go back to work.

2

It was foggy almost the whole way, beginning in Toledo, and it was after midnight by the time Guerin reached Washington. He went straight to his apartment on Fessendon in the Northwest District, where he lived alone by choice in spite of the fact that his employer-guardians generally preferred that single officers double up with their peers—not only as a check on potential defectors, but because the Firm psychologists felt it helped to ameliorate their inordinate alienation. The dampness, running to a cold now that mixed with the fatigue, was beginning to gnaw into his viscera and he left the luggage in the car and went up to the kitchen to start the coffee. Once it was perking, he telephoned the night duty officer for his section and reported in. He was forced to wait because even this routine call was funnelled through the scrambler.

'Guerin, Section L, Sub 1, Fifth Component, attached McNeely, reporting in residence.'

'Right, Guerin ... report DDP for referral 9.00 am., thank you.'

He repeated, 'Thank you,' automatically before he hung up, but it felt distinctly like thanking a recorded message.

The coffee was imported mocha, expensive, and one of the few indulgences he allowed himself. He poured a brandy to go with it, putting the bottle far back out of reach because he might need a tranquillizer later and had good reason to know they did not mix. It was impossible to repress a mournful smile at that kind of strained compendium of weakness and control he had just put together. But it was very necessary; the night duty officer might have already reported his presence to whomever it was that wanted him and the phone could ring and he would be on his way out to the Firm in fifteen minutes, in his car or someone else's. They were observant men and it would not do to have them find out.

August or no, it was cold enough in Washington to put steam in the radiator. He settled down by it with the coffee and some homework, a technical journal in Spanish about rural development in Bolivia. With that in hand it seemed unlikely he would need any tranquillizers.

24

The guard handed back his identification card and saluted.

'Hope you had a nice vacation, Mr Guerin.'

'Thanks, Tommy, it was okay.'

This was the third checkpoint he had encountered since entering the building. He had known all the guards by their first names, but of course his pass card had been perused as thoroughly as if he had been a total stranger. He put it back in his handkerchief pocket for easy access and started down the hall to his left.

'Beg pardon, Mr Guerin, straight ahead.'

'What?'

'Straight ahead for Mr Hammerle's office.'

'I'm not going there. Duty man said last night to report to DD for Plans.'

'Sorry, sir, but I have it right here.' He flourished his clip board. 'Must have been countermanded. There's a "no pass" for Deputy Director and an "expedite" to Mr Hammerle's component in 29A North Annex.'

'Tommy, what do you think would happen if I went to Deputy Director anyway, by mistake?'

The Guard looked nervous but he managed a thin smile. 'I don't know about you, but I'd probably wind up on Guam or Okinawa.'

Guerin seemed to be weighing that and the guard tried piling on sweet reasonableness. 'He's new, you know, so maybe he don't want anybody seeing his face that don't have to.'

'Doesn't want me to recognize him as the man who eats Greek cheese and tomatoes for lunch in the commissary every day.'

The guard laughed at that for what, Guerin assumed, were reasons of his own. He was already on his way when he had said it, straight ahead for Hammerle, whoever that was.

The business about the DDP annoyed him, because he

could remember a time when security had been considerably less formal and more reasonable. In the last year or two the day-to-day paranoia which more or less went with the job had insidiously become something rather more than half-mad. Whereas formerly they had joked about security and all its attendant absurdities, in fact had taken some pride in living with it and surviving it, the laughter had stopped and no one seemed to know why. Nothing Guerin could put his finger on, certainly, but that might only be because he avoided infrastructural politics of all kinds. The Service was factionalizing, that was the truth of it, you could feel it everywhere, and yet the how and the why eluded him.

The halls were long, empty and silent, their impersonality totalled by the fact that the doors bore no names. Only the sheer massiveness of the building gave it any substance at all.

Hammerle's office was pretty much like all the others at the operational level, Guerin thought, until he caught sight of the grim Goya and Velasquez prints outraging the modern functionalism of the rest of it. He hoped his assignment would not have anything to do with putting Don Juan back on the throne of Spain. The secretary, too, was grim, and axe-faced, a long-wearing veteran of the civil service system. It was by now several minutes after nine and she glanced at her desk clock as she greeted him.

'Go right in, please, he's waiting for you,' she said, without trying to disguise the disapproval in her voice.

Guerin smiled pleasantly and nodded. He reached for the handle just as the door was yanked open from the inside. Hammerle was there, obviously on the prod for him.

'Oh, you're here. Come in.'

A military man, Guerin guessed at first sight. As he pressed past him he looked closely at his suit—imitation

Ivy-League, not quite frayed or careless enough for the real thing. Might be West Point, but certainly not a 'good school' type otherwise. Greying brush cut, the eyes black on unsullied white and deep set. Formidable man, probably. Voice used to giving orders, and the way the words were clipped off meant they had not often been disobeyed. The Firm was run generally by the Eastern Establishment and if you worked your way up to a command position without that background you had one of two things to offer in quantity, intelligence or ruthlessness.

'I don't want to be interrupted,' Hammerle said to his secretary, before following him into the room.

That stride settled it—military. Guerin did not like them generally, although there were times on a dangerous run when they were preferable to the more civilized majority. He picked up the customary folder from the desk in front of him without its being proffered.

'Were you ever on China station?' Hammerle asked him abruptly.

'No. Never been out there at all except to Japan as a student on vacation.' He wondered why he had been asked that. Hammerle would have gone over his folder with extreme care. The mere mention of it would have some provocative, if illogical, connotation these days, since the 'Element' was generally thought to have originated on Taiwan. Guerin had heard somewhere that over at State they referred to them as 'Les Chinoises' (which was only typical of State), because of their curious love-hate kind of symbiosis with the Reds on the mainland. Anyway, if it was intended as some sort of feeler he had evidently failed it on his part, for the subject was changed with equal abruptness.

'It's a take-out mission. Cuba. The agent is there now, waiting. You'll find all the geographical detail in the folder as per usual, except that it ought to be considerably more refined than usual.' He pushed it across and Guerin read

27

the code name 'Mercator' on the cover. 'This is crucial, absolutely. I can't impress that upon you too much.'

Guerin looked up in surprise. 'I don't understand, sir.'

Hammerle stared through him. 'What?'

'Why this isn't being handled by the Miami resident. If the agent is already waiting and it's priority.'

'It is priority; it's not routine. The resident is routine. Thought I'd made that clear.'

Guerin did not answer. He waited.

'She's set her own conditions. You'll have a week.' He got up and lit a cigarette without offering one. Turning to the big window, he lapsed into silence. Under certain conditions you could see deer in the woods from high up on this side of the building. Hammerle would be a hunter.

She, according to the folder, was Julia Fernandez, a Cuban national, thought to have been born in the United States to a Puerto Rican Negro mother and a father who was a Sephardic Jew. Secretary in the Ministry of the Interior. Age: thirty-three. Recruited three years four months, active two years seven months. Total payments in the neighbourhood of twenty-two hundred dollars. Low. That meant they had something on her, probably. An odd type, Guerin thought, to be involved in anything really critical.

'Something important that isn't down there. You won't find it down anywhere, of course,' Hammerle said, without turning, 'and that is that the agent is bringing out what we really want—papers. The agent herself is secondary, valuable but secondary. And also, she's ... proven herself undependable.'

'Specifically, am I to regard her as friendly or not?'

'You're to save her if possible, her testimony could be valuable to us. If she is co-operative, you will certainly co-operate with her. But if absolutely necessary, you're also authorized to waste her.' He said it without changing

28

his stance, his gaze or in any way altering his well-modulated voice.

'I'm sorry, Mr Hammerle, I don't do ...' It sounded so absurd he could hardly get it out ... 'that kind of work. You must have seen my file. I've never been asked to.'

'I've seen your file, of course.' Hammerle turned back from the window and, for a moment, fixed those excessive eyes on him. It was a gesture, so calculated that Guerin read it instantly and lost his fear of the man. Look at the way the head is slightly tilted, he told himself. The real ones don't indulge in stagecraft. Hammerle was an 'actor'. That explained a lot about the things he had said and the way he was saying them.

Suddenly Guerin was confronted with a sunburst of a smile, an almost totally disarming smile. 'I wasn't ordering you to execute anyone, you know. Simply authorizing you to authorize it should extraordinary circumstances arrive. You won't even be going in, yourself. Political situation won't allow for the risk.'

'Not even when the material is this vital?'

Hammerle sat down again, looking patient and rather confidential, as if between two employees of the same unreasonable taskmaster. 'The political restrictions are of long-standing and come directly from the White House. There's no reason to think that they've even been apprised of the particular situation that has necessitated this mission.'

'What's in the papers?'

Without hesitation he was told: 'You won't be told.'

'But you're asking me to make terminal judgments on the spot. Yet how can I evaluate the situation if I don't even know what I'm to bring back?'

The older man ground out his cigarette with perhaps more energy than was required for the simple separation of fire and air, but he had obviously decided to get along with Guerin for the purposes of this interview. 'Even the outcoming agent does not, or should not, know the contents of the material she's bringing.' He sighed. 'Of course that's unlikely under the circumstances.'

'I'd like to be frank, sir. There's a lot about this assignment I don't understand. And I don't think I'll find the answers in here.' He waved the folder. 'Things I think I should know, even if you can't tell me what the documents contain.'

Hammerle glanced at his desk clock. 'You may *ask* anything you wish.' Then he added, 'Within reason.'

Whatever that meant, Guerin ignored it. He wanted to know, 'Why weren't the documents simply photographed?'

'I can tell you that. The authenticity, aside from content, is a critical point here, therefore the paper, ink, fingerprints, signatures ... all bear analysing.'

'Is the agent doubling us?'

'Not necessarily. But originally we wanted her to stay on station. Her cover was tight as far as we knew and there was no reason to think she couldn't survive the recoil if she followed certain precautions. The documents weren't active and might not have been missed for some time. But she wouldn't do that. Either just before or after her move—I haven't been told myself, actually—she demanded that she be brought out too, as the price of the documents, so to speak.'

'Nervy girl. Why?'

'Yes.' His tone was flat, giving away nothing. 'Why did she want out? Usual paranoia, I suppose ... catches up with everybody. Maybe she just got tired of it all; she's not a professional, not even a very highly rated agent despite the fortuitousness of her location. You know our Cubans; they can't fight but they love to spy on each other, so there's no shortage of people. Only truth,' he added, with a weary smile that was intended to make you feel sorry for him.

30

'Any particular reason why I was chosen for the assignment?' Guerin had surprised himself in asking that.

'That's a curious question, Mr Guerin. I don't believe an agent's ever asked me before.' For a moment it looked as though the hard-line which began their conversation would come back, but then he relaxed again. 'I've stressed the importance of the mission, and your ratings are very high. You're a company man, you're on the Latin desk already, and McNeely speaks for you. Why not Guerin?'

'I see, thank you, sir.'

'See transportation next. They'll put you in Miami to-morrow. From there you make your own moves, but through the usual channels, of course. Everything will be available to you. The rest of the day you have for boning. Anything else?'

They shook hands, very firm on both sides, and Guerin went to the door.

As he opened it, Hammerle's voice, filled with solicitation, stopped him. 'I heard you were on vacation. Sorry, but if you're successful I'm sure the Director will be happy to authorize six weeks wherever you were.'

'Thanks, but I won't be going back.' He did not know why he had said that, either; it was meaningless as far as Hammerle was concerned, and only sounded petulant.

'Well, good luck ... Mercator.'

Guerin closed the door and went past the secretary, who was already starting to put through piled-up calls, without speaking. That was all right, secretaries at the Firm were used to not being spoken to. It was the price they paid for a life of adventure.

The anomalies of the interview, the nagging suspicions he felt about the assignment itself, suddenly none of that mattered now that he was running again. The nerves had improved already. Hammerle, after all, he might never even see again. The main thing was, he was committed to something, he felt alive, he could risk, risk, risk ...

31

'Hi again, Tommy.' He handed the guard his identification in order to get out.

3

Guerin made an appointment with Research for directly after lunch, then went down to the library where there were soundproof cubicles in which he could study the operational folder Hammerle had given him. He committed the contents to memory in an hour, not being a particularly 'quick study', and spent another hour acting upon the information he had absorbed.

A quarter of a mile walk to a distant wing of the plant took him to the armourer. He checked out a small automatic pistol and shoulder holster which had a note attached reminding the lendee that he must be sure to apply to Documents for the appropriate papers which would allow him to carry a concealed weapon. The pistol was primarily for use within the country itself and was authorized 'to guarantee safety while carrying and transporting vital and highly secret materials', and also in light of 'the well-known instability that characterizes the exile community in Southeastern Florida with which said agent must associate'. He smiled to himself at a description which was, in his own experience, wildly charitable. For use in the Caribbean or wherever else he was obliged to operate outside the borders of the continental United States he would be issued a machine pistol with flash-guard and silencer of a sort developed by the OSS during World War Two, but this would have to be picked up from the resident in Miami or Key West. If he wanted it.

'We don't issue chits for many of them,' the armourer

told him, indicating the order for the machine pistol. 'Beautiful piece of work, too, it's a shame.'

'Yes,' Guerin agreed, without enthusiasm. He did not particularly like guns or people who liked guns, especially not in his profession where they were more often the precipitator of difficulties than the resolution of them. The armourer, he had heard somewhere, was a twenty-year marine veteran, and he looked the part with his bullet head, creased and sunburned face, and a body that seemed to be attacking his civilian clothes out of regret. While he was filling in the papers required for the issuance of firearms under Section H. Subsection 7c, Paragraph 9 governing basic relationships between the Firm and its employees, Guerin was thinking with regret of the various European stations where he had served previously, and the lack of guns and bullet-headed, heavy-bearded lovers of guns that characterized that more civilized theatre of operations generally. Whereas, the Caribbean was bound to be full of types like the one in front of him.

'Those Cuban boys will all want one when they see yours,' the armourer said cheerfully. 'Too bad they're such a bunch of fuck-ups.'

'Yes,' Guerin replied on his way out, 'too bad.' He had learned a long time ago, when he was in the service himself, that you walked around Neanderthals until you rose above them. It was a kind of snobbery; he recognized that.

When he had gone, the armourer said to his assistant, who had just come in from the supply room with a crate of small calibre pistol ammunition, 'Snotty son-of-a-bitch!'

'Aren't they all?' the assistant, a Marine Lance Corporal in mufti, agreed.

'One of the fancy-school boys. Sometimes I think the Commies got the right idea about them.'

Guerin had decidedly mixed feelings about eating in the commissary. The food was terrible and, while far from

33

a gourmet, he probably would not be eating very well for the next month or so; but then, on the other hand, it was fast and if he hurried through his day the evening, no doubt his last in Washington for some time, might belong to him. He would have liked a free night out.

Striding through the halls worrying about it, he ran into an Englishman, an officer with the Firm whom he had met while stationed at the Consulate in Zagreb. The Englishman was something less than brilliant but extremely good-natured, and in the end that decided for the commissary.

Luncheon, aside from the unexpected improvement in the Shrimp Louis, was uneventful. They gossiped about the people they had known abroad, exchanged rumours about what was going on 'in house' and in Washington generally and the Englishman told a funny story about a friend of his in the Foreign Office with six children who had tried to pass as a homosexual in order to advance his career.

Guerin was feeling good when he left. On his way out he spotted a man named Sanford, an old friend, one of the few people in the Firm with whom he had ever had a real relationship. He was seated by himself at a small table near the main entrance. Guerin had just excused himself from the Englishman, who had the time to sit over a second cup of coffee, and was headed for the cashier, so he hailed his friend from some distance away. At first Sanford did not see him, but then, when he did look up, his face clouded, he rose from the table, almost knocking over a glass, and hurried out the door, barely pausing to slap down some money with his cheque as he went by the register. Guerin slowed his pace and made no attempt to catch up. He was deeply puzzled and could think of no reason for Sanford to behave in that way, but in the Firm you did not wear your heart on your sleeve or press other people to explain themselves. Whatever it was about, the answer was lost to him for now and he should have forgotten about it. Still, it affected his concentration the rest of the afternoon.

When he got to Research he found they had already prepared a recommended set of punch cards and arranged them neatly and alphabetically in a small portable file.

'A new service,' the technical librarian said. He was a mild-faced little man, much like librarians on the outside were supposed to look.

'So I notice,' Guerin replied absently, while he flipped through the labels on the punch cards. In sum, they provided a comprehensive on everything having to do remotely with the assignment he was about to undertake, from the flora of rural Cuba in the area where the outcoming agent was to wait for transport, to a biography of her life. What was not there, of course, was anything about the secret that a lot of them would be risking their lives to bring out with her.

'You used to have to look up your own.'

'What?'

'I said, you used to have to get your own tapes and cards.'

'I know, I've been here a number of years.'

'Oh, sorry.'

'I think I liked it better the other way.'

'Why is that?'

'Because this way some bureaucrat, present company accepted, can pre-select me dead. Respectfully, I prefer to decide for myself what information is vital to a mission.'

'I'm sorry, sir, but the Director himself authorized this new service. I'm sure you could obtain permission to compile your own programme if you wished.'

'Run this one.'

'If you would prefer—'

'No, run this one, please.'

With an irritated toss of his head, the librarian went off to programme the mission. Guerin felt miserable. Everything he had said was true, but of course reckless and unnecessary. This predilection for taking everybody on, even when there was some justification for it, was going to be fatal. Word would get around and they would run a check on him. If the Firm ever discovered that he was seeing a psychiatrist who was not one of their own, their solution could well be something more drastic than discharge. He had been around long enough now to know about that. So the armourer was one thing, but now this inoffensive little librarian. Nerves, obviously. It was then it occurred to him that the incident with Sanford had perhaps been more unsettling than he had realized. Why?

'We'll run the Intellofax first, if you don't mind, Mr Guerin.'

No, he would not mind.

He did not mind the computers either, in fact preferred them to the sort of team briefing that was standard when he had first entered the Firm. This process took exactly fifty-nine minutes and pre-selected pieces of information were fed through teaching machines so that he was grilled on the data he had received and when he answered incorrectly it was automatically reprogrammed and fed back to him. There was no question about its being a more efficient system in spite of what he had said to the librarian. He had never handled precisely this sort of takeout mission before and here was a statistical analysis of what had and could go wrong, telling, for instance, that twenty-one per cent of the failures under approximately matching circumstances were due to geographical and/or climatological errors, with a breakdown of same, twenty-three per cent because of an agent being doubled, and so on.

He asked for tapes dealing with Julia Fernandez to be run more than once. The photographs revealed her to be not pretty but unusual and attractive, with high, almost oriental cheekbones and large, quite extraordinary eyes. Her hair was long, the skin dark, close to Negroid, but the features were aquiline. She was tall for a Cuban, although of course she was not that, strictly speaking, and her nose and mouth were a trifle too large. Still, the only beautiful female agent Guerin had ever seen was a prostitute employed by the GRU in Vienna and no one there had ever considered her a truly political animal.

The biography stated that Julia's exact birthplace was somehow not known for certain, but she had grown up in New York and enjoyed both American and Cuban citizenship. Her father, a musician from Havana, had abandoned his wife and family when she was only seven. Her childhood was poverty-stricken and she herself had left home at sixteen. However, by working as a waitress and then a singer in smalltime nightclubs, she had put herself through a year at CCNY. Later she had performed in Atlantic City, Miami, Puerto Rico and Havana, where she had eventually settled down with relatives of her father. She had never married but there followed a long list of men thought to have been lovers, one of whom had been executed in the Cabana. There was also a note to the effect that she was unusually reticent in discussing these matters. The official implication seemed to be that verbal discretion in the area of sexuality was only another side to an independence of mind which made her a not always dependable agent.

Curious, Guerin thought to himself, that there was nothing about her motivation except for a notation about the twenty-two hundred dollars which had been mentioned in the folder and deposited for her in a Key West Bank under a Firm cover account. There might well be something in an earlier item about her being suspect by the Revolution during her first two years on the island because of her relationship with the executed man.

When the briefing was complete, Guerin asked that the machines be turned off and he be left alone for a moment. He sat back in the swivel chair with his head resting on the computer behind him and his eyes tightly closed. He always needed a moment like this to absorb what he had experienced, to sort it out. He ran other biographies through his mind and realized that when motivational information was scanty it invariably meant the sub-agent was being kept on the string by blackmail. Somehow, the most hardened officers were self-conscious about putting that into the file, unless of course the person being black-mailed was really important, in which case it could be regarded as a coup and something to be proud of. Hammerle had said the Fernandez girl was being baulky, had thrown a wrench into their plans somewhere along the way by demanding to be brought out with her information. Well, it was making a picture now. As for her being a relatively attractive girl, that meant for him only a series of functional judgments such as would she be vain, were there present lovers to be considered, exactly how susceptible was she to men in general ... none of it having any implications beyond the fact that it was his job to carry out a dangerous and politically sensitive mission with a minimum of risk and an absolute certainty of success.

'Thank you, it was a good programme,' he told the librarian on the way out. The man did not respond, but Guerin was no longer worrying about him. Julia Fernandez had somehow started him thinking of a totally different sort of girl, one he had not seen now in three months. He felt a desperate yearning to spend this one free night in her company before all the grief began again.

The moment he got back to the apartment he called her. Phyllis worked for a Congressman from Illinois; she was clever and sorority house-pretty and had a laugh like broken crystal, but managed to be warm and sane enough when it counted. Like most of the single girls in Washington she lived with two roommates who were always getting in the way:

'Who?'

'Guerin, Stephen.'

'Oh ... oh, just a minute, please.'

That would be the one called Maggie, a short plump Bryn Mawr graduate who insisted on being afraid of him, as though he were some kind of tough cop. In the beginning it had been mildly amusing but now it was only annoying. In theory, of course, they were not even supposed to know what he did.

'Stephen, how nice to hear from you,' Phyllis's voice came over, bright and buoyant. Nevertheless, it was a jab —he knew her that well.

'Yes, well, I'm sorry it's been so long. I've been out of town, seeing my children.'

'How nice for you.'

'Before that I was ... well, you know, on assignment.'

'Yes, I know how that goes.'

'I'm getting a lot of con tonight, how come?'

'You sound a little stiff yourself, as a matter of fact.'

'I'm in one of my formal moods,' he snapped impatiently, 'now why don't you level with me.'

'Why did you call me, Stephen?'

'Why? Do I have to have an appointment? Because I wanted to see you! Maybe have dinner. I'm going out again tomorrow ... on business. Right?'

'Well ... I can't. Tonight.'

'All right.'

'Stephen?'

'Yes.'

'Not tomorrow night, either. I'm engaged.' She added, 'to someone else.'

Stephen said, 'Oh ... well, I didn't think it was to me,'

39

and immediately regretted its lameness. They had been much too close for that sort of thing. 'Look, this is a hell of a way to let me know.'

'I know. I feel guilty as all hell. I'm sorry.'

'Okay. I wish you well.'

'Oh, Christ!' she said. 'I really am sorry. To tell you like this on the phone ... is rotten.' He suspected she was going to cry. She was not a girl to cry easily, so he accepted the compliment as partial payment. 'I know how you hate and distrust talking on the phone anyway.' She tried to turn that into a joke but failed tearfully.

'Part of the paranoia that goes with the job.' He hesitated. 'Let's break this off now, Phil, and I wish you luck. He's a lucky guy.'

She really was crying now. 'Don't use cliches like that —you hate cliches. It was only your—job. You know how I felt ... it wasn't you ... I just couldn't ...'

He hung up gently. Anything more would be demeaning to both of them. It might be that he had loved her.

Guerin opened a new bottle of brandy as the measure of his despair. He sat back and wondered idly if it might not be worth it to take up with several girls at once just to drive the Security boys bonkers trying to check them all out at once? A reasonable estimate would be that the sub rosa clearance check on Phyllis alone had cost the taxpayers several thousand dollars and God knows how many man-hours, and she had already had one from the FBI because of her position with the Congressman. He consoled himself that the phone call just concluded had cost the government almost as much as it had him.

He moved over to sit in the window casement and looked out. Summer had returned and the city lay in a heavy lavender twilight, with streetlamps bursting consecutively into luminous strings of globes over the home-going traffic on the boulevards below. Guerin loved Washington, with all its problems. A city without much colour or immediacy, he thought, but without pretensions too, and with a feeling of continuity about it that denied the fragmented rest of the nation. You could see the history of the Republic in the simple choice of building materials.

The phone rang in on his reflections, and he was not ungrateful. He only hoped it would be a familiar voice.

'Hello, Mr Guerin?'

'Yes.'

'My name is McIntyre.' The speaker, Guerin knew, was pressing slightly against his nose in order to distort the voice quality. 'I was with the State Department when we met a couple of years ago in Rome. Do you remember?'

'Yes, of course. Nice to hear from you.'

The caller also knew that Security, were they listening, did not like to check out people at State, because that institution had its own Security and all of them over there had little brief for the Firm.

'You said at the time we should look each other up if ever I got back to Washington. I'm in private business now.'

'Congratulations.'

'I was wondering, could we have dinner?'

'As a matter of fact, I was just wishing for someone to have dinner with.'

The man on the phone thought it was very lucky that they were both looking for 'someone to have dinner with'. He named a restaurant; Guerin agreed immediately and hung up.

He hurried into the bathroom and started the shower, taking the brandy with him. He was curious and worried. The whole business on the phone had been silly and, as a matter of fact, not even done well. Sanford was better than that, he knew from experience.

4

The Hound and Hare was some distance out along the Potomac, a small English-style inn, all brass and dark wood, with tables set among the trees overlooking the river. Even by the dullish candlelight it would be comparatively simple to spot a tag. Guerin looked around casually; it had been chosen for that reason without a doubt. Also, the fact that Sanford was not yet there was indication of security concern, the late arriver having the option of checking the place out before he enters. Guerin found these musings unsettling; a lot of his fellow professionals engaged in such games as a matter of course, to keep in form presumably, but he had never known Sanford to be one of them. No, Sanford was eminently sane; he had kept his sense of humour up to now.

There was no maître d'hôtel and Guerin himself had taken a table behind a tree which gave him a visual advantage over anyone coming out of the restaurant proper on to the terrace. He had Sanford dead to rights coming in, and was both pleased and embarrassed by it. 'Sandy!'

The small man turned threequarters and Guerin could see the frown, quickly wiped before he came straight on. So he was not above the game, either. Another disappointment. The place being nearly empty, the waitress was over before Sanford was seated and took their order for drinks. Both men were silent until she was well gone.

'It's been almost a year, Sandy.'

'Nearly that.'

Guerin waited for him to say more. The face across the table was pale, delicately etched and intelligent. Now it stared down at the river impassively.

'Stephen ... I'm sorry for all this melodrama. It's not my style, that you know.'

'I know. But it's a nice little place. I'll bring a girl here next time.'

'I'm reasonably certain it's not a "running tap". Feebies get uncomfortable around grass and trees. I don't know why that is.'

Guerin knew the Bureau, as well as other security agencies, kept certain Washington establishments, particularly restaurants, primed for bugging, and that they moved it around sometimes just on general principles, but he had never concerned himself with it and thought stories of the extensiveness of the practice were probably exaggerated. Anyway, you simply could not afford to worry about such things or you would drown in your own precautions. He was disturbed to see that Sandy no longer understood that.

There was another long silence. Finally Sanford went on record about the cuisine. 'Especially the seafood. The Dover Sole—get that.'

'To hell with the seafood. To hell with food in general. Right?'

'Okay ...'

'The burden's on you, Sandy. I don't know what's going on. And I'm afraid I don't have an awful lot of time. I'm going out tomorrow.'

'Where?'

Guerin noted the eagerness in the other man's face. He had actually leaned across the table to ask.

'You know better. Christ, what's got into you in a year?'

Sanford leaned back and gave a short, unconvincing laugh. 'Pieces have started to come off, I guess. Maybe you'd better recommend that off-campus shrinker you've got.'

'The way you're acting, I'm damned sorry I ever told you about that.'

'You were drunk.'

'You were the only person in the Firm, in the world probably, I would have admitted that to, drunk or sober. If you're going into a bloody crackup, you'll take me with you.'

'I'm not really cracking. I have rational reasons for my ... fears.'

'They all say that. Jesus.'

Guerin had been seeing his private psychiatrist secretly on and off for the past year. The diagnosis had been quite ordinary, or would have been for anyone else— anxiety neurosis consisting of a mixed bag of hypocondria, neurasthenia, hysteria, etc., in short, 'a garden variety neurotic, a typical modern young man,' the doctor had summarized, presumably making his own kind of joke. But the Firm, of course, had its own thoroughly approved right-thinking psychiatric staff, and anyone violating the rules in this respect would be judged an extreme security risk and subject to the severest discipline. Perhaps at the hands of that same staff. He was being honest when he said he regretted having told Sanford.

'Stephen, I called you because ... for no other reason than I wanted to talk to someone I trusted.'

Guerin, lost in private thought, took his turn at staring down at the lights bouncing off the turgid, muddy snake below. The waitress brought their drinks, his a rare Irish whiskey, clean and cold, and he shifted his eyes to the amber reflections in the glass, thinking what a struggle it was to keep his life away from work, and lately in it, as pure and uncomplicated as this choice of liquids. 'We all have that problem,' he responded finally. Sanford started to say something but he cut him off: 'Christ, that phone call was lousy, amateur night ...' He was surprised by his own embittered tone of voice. 'If anyone had Guerin under surveillance they'd put a whole goddamned section on him after that.'

'Are you under surveillance?'

Guerin sipped from the drink, put it down and shrugged. 'Not unless you happened to hit a routine check. Or the other side's interested in me for some reason I don't know about.'

'I'm not concerned about Hostiles.'

'Oh?'

'I'm in trouble, Stephen, with the "Element".'

Guerin did not reply immediately, then he looked away and snorted. 'No such thing. No such bloody goddamned thing.'

'You know better.'

'Then you've done something incredibly stupid. Like joining the opposition.'

Sanford again laughed without sincerity, a rasping, unpleasant sound. 'You think I've been doubled—I'm going to defect?'

'My turn to say "you know better". I'm talking domestic —when you said we'll leave the Hostiles out I accepted that.'

'All right. You're talking about the "Bourse". But if I'd joined I couldn't very well tell you, could I?'

'That's what I said, they don't exist. Boys get bored, little boys, and we have them in the Firm ... they play at games like this "Bourse" and "Element" business, whatever the hell those mean ... Just what *do* they mean, Sandy?' He realized that he was badgering a friend who had asked him for help, but now that he had started it was difficult to stop. The very subject was an anathema.

Sandy took him seriously, however. 'As I understand it, and of course there's no way of being absolutely sure about any of this, but the "Element" was started or founded or organized, or whatever, by or around Admiral Quarry back in ... oh, I guess the early fifties. At first it was just a kind of correspondence club of like-minded

45

gentlemen. You know, hard-liners. You're familiar with Quarry, aren't you?'

'Only that he's dead.'

'Not entirely. But as I was saying, he goes all the way back to our parent service during the war. Evidently hated the Hostiles even then, when they were allies. In the thirties they say he was big in government and financial circles, so when the trouble started he naturally got into our field during the "Oh So Social" era—gone but unlamented. How in hell he had time to become an admiral, I don't know. Maybe during World War One. Anyway, the story is, when someone tried to alert the Old Man way back then that there was a clandestine faction forming right inside his own service, and of a particular political hue, he stopped puffing on that damned pipe just long enough to dismiss it airily with, "Oh, that Quarry Element". *Noblesse Oblige*. Of course, his brother was at the height of his power then so it must have seemed inconsequential. But nobody's done anything about the "Element" since and it just keeps growing.'

Guerin groaned involuntarily. 'You mean to tell me that even the name of the goddamned abomination is in the hands of rumour: that it's based on an anecdote?'

The other man looked hurt. 'The origins, you asked me about. There's no doubt anywhere that it does exist. And that it can punish. They're not soft, those people, and they don't like people who are. Strongly authoritarian. They want the world in a certain image ...'

A question had been forming in Guerin's mind the reason for which he could not logically justify in that he desperately wanted out of the entire conversation, but he asked it nevertheless: 'Does any of this have to do with anti-semitism, Sandy?'

'I didn't say that. I didn't even suggest it.'

'No, you never do, even on those occasions when you've suffered from it, but I'm asking just the same. Since you came to me as a friend.' Sandy seemed embarrassed by the question and Guerin had a hard time imagining why.

'It's true ... al ... always true,' he almost stammered, 'that when you get people of that orientation and, I guess, ideology, together there will be a few of them—but no, that isn't it. I was telling you about the histories. The "Bourse" was originally called, I'm told, the "Luft Circle". And I suppose its principal reason for coming into being was only to combat the intentions of the "Element". Because they are certainly people willing to accommodate, to press for and encourage solutions, even in areas outside of our own specialty. But getting back to the names ... In this case, too, it may have been someone named Luft, but one esoteric theory is it was from a mis-spelling of the World War One flying manoeuvre called the Lufbery Circle and was pinned on them derisively by some grizzled old flyboy as meaning they chased their own tails ...'

'I'm sorry I asked,' Guerin cut in brusquely. 'What I wanted to say earlier was that the rest of us, whatever these people think, are professionals. We have careers to guard and records to keep and grown up lives to live. You should know that I wouldn't be interested.'

'You're patronizing me, Stephen.'

'I'm sorry.'

'You've conceded their existence, at least. I guess I should be happy for small favours. Maybe someday, before it's too late, I can convince you how serious it is.'

'Maybe you could if you'd level with me. You do have a wife and two well-set-up boys I'm very fond of, so I have some vested interest in your immortality.'

'Would you talk to McNeely for me. He likes you and you've performed well for him. I want to go "in house" for a while.'

'Why?'

'I've been out on China station and around. Quarryites, whether you want to believe it or not, run things out

47

there these days. They're powerful and aggressive, the "Bourse" is puny by comparison. You never know when you're given an assignment whether it's legitimate or maybe just intended to take you off the rolls. I mean it.'

'I know you do,' Guerin sighed, and made a gesture of resignation with his hands. 'I can't do it until I come off this run, Sandy. I leave in six hours. Then I'll be glad to.'

Sanford took a menu from an adjoining table and studied it over-zealously. 'I should have approached you sooner.'

'In the commissary at lunch wouldn't have been too late.' The tone was mild enough but there was still reproof implied for that embarrassing bit of melodrama earlier, and Sanford read it correctly.

'I was trying to protect you.'

'It's no secret that we've been friends. That's bound to be locked in the computers somewhere.'

The waitress came and took their order, dinner arrived, went down and was taken away with indifference all around. What was noted, but only in their rapid passing, were two bottles of Pouilley Fouissé which were recklessly poured after the whisky. The truth was, Guerin, while concerned about what he took to be either his friend's disorientation or imprudence, was by dinnertime running his own mission through his head. He always did this, and at great length, on the night before starting out. He did not consider himself either quick or clever, but he was thorough. He did his benedictions.

'I'm getting a new assignment myself tomorrow.'

'What?' Guerin asked. 'I'm sorry.'

'What would you think if I told you you were going to the Caribbean station tomorrow morning, that the man who is sending you is Hammerle and it's a take-out mission of some kind?'

There was something almost sly about the way it was said, but he had Guerin's interest back. 'How the hell could you know all that? You've just scared the shit out of me, you know it. How could you?'

'I'm trying to demonstrate that there's no such thing as security any more, not like we used to have it. The different interests make it their business to keep track of everybody.'

'Is that supposed to make me feel better, because it doesn't. Anyway, I'm a neutral, dammit! I don't belong to anybody and I think all this silly factionalism is destructive and stupid and childish. I don't want anything to do with it. Clear?'

'No one's ever tried to recruit you?'

Guerin looked hard. 'Not until now.'

Sanford stared at him for a moment, then turned his attention to the remnants of his salad. 'I don't know where my tour will take me, or even who's running it. We haven't been able to find out because it's in *their* hands. Take my chances, I guess.'

Guerin was irritated by the way the other man had gone right by his challenge. He had not really believed that Sanford was recruiting him for one of the factions, except maybe by inference, and he had thought he would get mad about it.

They had gone through the food in comparative silence. Guerin had eaten quickly; he was anxious for it to be over. When it was, he insisted on paying the cheque, insisted too hard perhaps out of guilt and regret. Surprisingly, Sandy said he would not be leaving just yet, that he had still another meeting that night.

Guerin raised an eyebrow. 'I thought you said you weren't going to work until tomorrow—it's after eleven.'

Sanford smiled, but with that certain melancholy Guerin always associated with three thousand years of ethnic tragedy. 'I've got to keep moving just to stay alive.'

'I'm sorry, Sandy,' he said, as he rose to leave. 'I'll do what I can the moment I get back. Maybe you'll draw six weeks in Philadelphia or New Brunswick tomorrow.'

'Maybe.' The smile, melancholy or no, faded. 'Stephen, you can't stay neutral. You won't be allowed to.'

Guerin remained standing by the table, looking down almost unpleasantly. 'That's why we had dinner?'

'No. It's simply an impression. But your assignment ... well, Hammerle's one of "them". Or at least a sympathizer.'

'How do you know?'

'Please, I have it—I know.'

'They have no reason, assuming what you say is true, to set me up.'

'No, you're neutral.'

'Goodnight, Sandy.'

Guerin went home with the hope of five hours sleep. As he left the restaurant a grey Ford in the parking area discharged one of its two occupants, then followed him out of the driveway and part of the way back to Washington. They were easily identifiable by virtue of their very colourlessness as agents of the Bureau. So his friend had been right about that possibility, at least. Also, he was forced to consider the purported bond of sympathy that was said to extend between many of the Bureau people and the 'Element'. He considered it but in the end he rejected it as irrelevant, or unprovable at best. Logically it was a routine check, or even a training exercise. As for the rest of this evening, Sanford evidently had the endemic disease; he felt bad about it but there was not anything he could do.

5

The flight down was in a bucket seat in the back of a creaking Globemaster delivering ice cream and sundries to the naval personnel of Key West and Guantanamo.

Guerin liked it this way, because military people generally regarded employees of the Firm as something exotic
and unfathomable, and on the whole left them alone.
Except for a young ensign who brought him coffee and
kept a close but deferential watch out of the corners of
his eyes, he was free to read or watch the countryside
below, whereas on a commercial flight the whole trip
could be consumed telling an endless string of silly lies to
some excited tourist.

He liked the Caribbean; not doing business there, but
physically. His parents had often wintered somewhere on
its periphery when he was a child, so it was an old
love. If he had anything against Castro it was a simple
matter of disturbing the peace in that quarter of the
world. Watching for the first appearance of the crystalline
blue-green water that would presage the tropics, he could
feel the blood already beginning to run high. No more
nerves now—he was working.

They put him down at the Opa Laka Naval Air Station
outside of Miami. A full flood of sweet warm air that
came when they threw open the door in the back of the
plane cheered him enormously. The ensign helped him
down before the ground crew got there and then saluted
smartly.

'Goodbye, sir. I hope you have a successful ... time.'

Guerin thanked him, and smiled to himself as he strode
briskly away towards the communications building. The
ensign watched him go: a slim, self-contained man in his
thirties, wearing a lightweight khaki suit, a blue shirt with
long collars and a wide-striped tie. He was carrying a
briefcase, like any young broker or lawyer. The face, oddly
enough, he could not remember at all—a very ordinary
face. The ensign shook his head; the pilot had told him
they were bringing some kind of cop or spy along but

this one had turned out to be rather bland. He reminded himself to put it in his next letter home anyway, although of course he would have to dress it up a bit.

Guerin was offered a ride into town but preferred to call for a cab and pick it up a block or two away. On principle he always severed connections with the military as soon as possible. Fortunately, being an officer, he had that option.

The cabdriver was a garrulous old man and talked all the way in, but he drove with skill and the required daring. They skittered through late afternoon traffic on Flagler Street like a dragonfly, though in the heart of the exile district on Southwest Eighth the crowds used the sidewalks and streets interchangeably, making progress slower.

'Ever see so many greasers in your life?' the driver asked him.

'What?' Guerin had been trying to remember what he had heard about the Miami resident.

'These Cubans. Exiles. Jesus, they're overrunnin' the town. We got more 'an New York. I used to hack up there but the spics ruined it where I was, so I come down here. An' my health, I got sinus trouble and my old lady's got arthritis, and this is great around here, the weather is. But now we got all these spics. They don't work, unless the women get something, and sit around like this—look at 'em—in these joints here yakin' and yakin'. Big talkers but no workers. Government tries to send 'em around the country but they won't go and we gotta support 'em on the relief roles. Ya know why? They're all aristocrats. Even the shoeshine boys all tell ya a story about how cosy they had it once upon a time back home.'

'Let me off at the next corner,' Guerin told him abruptly. It was not that he was offended, he had not even been listening, but he wanted to approach the resident's office on foot as a matter of proper procedure.

The cabbie, however, decided it was a reproof and kept a concerned eye on the tip. 'I guess, if ya think about it, they can't help it though, can they—after what that bastard Castro done to 'em.'

Guerin paid the man off and left him happy, if only not to draw attention to himself. He liked walking in the barrio, liked the smell of angry black coffee and strong tobacco, the liquid sound of the language, especially in laughter, liked the guayaberra shirts and the broad loose hips of the women. It was unfortunate, he thought, that he liked Cubans generally.

The Cal-Way Corporation was housed in a small building that was brighter and more modern than anything else on the street. The Firm's weakness for comfort and efficiency, he told himself. Probably everybody in Miami knew who the resident was, anyway. Once one of the exiles was let in on a cover, it was blown. An agent returning from an extremely dangerous clandestine mission out of this station had told Guerin bitterly that you were lucky if the kids did not make up songs about you and follow you down the street singing them.

It was encouraging to find the Cal-Way secretary a middle-aged woman, more efficient-looking than pretty. His experience with various agencies and embassies around the world had convinced him that you never got enough of what you needed from the ones who tended to hire attractive women. That was all right, of course, as long as people's lives were not at stake.

'Hello, Mercator,' the big man greeted him, as he was passed into the inner office, 'glad to have you aboard.' He moved forward with a trace of a limp.

Guerin shook hands with him. The resident's palms were damp and he found himself unconsciously wiping his hands on his pants as he sat down.

'Iris, get some booze in here and some ice.' He turned to Guerin before he sat down. 'What'll you have? We only got bourbon, I think.'

That turned out to be true and Guerin accepted only out of politeness; he knew he would pay for it when he went out into the high humidity again.

They sized each other up carefully through the amenities and while they were waiting for the drinks that would signal the beginning of business.

'I'm a Southern boy, I guess that's why we always got bourbon. Can't stand the heat though, never have—hope the air conditioning isn't too cold in here, is it?'

Guerin's eyes scanned the papers on the cluttered desk, all of them upside down to him but readable nevertheless, because it was something he had trained himself to do. Those which did not have to do specifically with his mission were fake, they went with the cover, Charles E. Middlebrook, Attorney at Law, President of Cal-Way Corporation. None of them would have told you exactly what Cal-Way Corporation did or why it even existed. As for Middlebrook himself, Guerin tended to accept the Southern derivation but noted the accent scarcely existed. Must have been out of the South for long periods of time—a good guess would be another career serviceman. The way he moved, and particularly the way he sat down, inclined Guerin to the Navy. He was about fifty with blond hair easing gracefully into light grey, good-natured looking and yet he would have to be pretty hard to hold this particular assignment.

'This little gal you're taking out, I used to run her myself, only now it's under Virgil in Key West. He works under me, only his reports on this deal go right by me straight to Washington, if you know how that is.'

Guerin nodded sympathetically: he knew.

'The girl—we called her Estrellita at this end—not too bad looking, although the only pictures I ever had she

54

didn't know were being taken, so you can't rightly tell. Anyway, she's been part of a component down there that was never worth a goddamn, most of them. She was well located, Ministry of the Interior, for Christ's sake, but no aggressiveness and apparently not even reliable.'

'Why?'

'Doesn't say on her rap sheet—don't you know?'

'No. But I'm surprised you don't, if you've been running her.'

'She wasn't recruited during my time; I inherited her along with the rest of these idiots in her component— clerks and typists, a cop, a priest, or at least he says he's a priest, some people from the various embassies. But it's not much. If the Firm is relying on what goes through here for its beat on Havana, I'd say the future's not bright for Southeast Florida. Obviously they don't, but I remember when a resident was a resident.'

'Where was that?'

'China station mostly.' Middlebrook spread out his large hands on the desk and seemed to be considering the state of the cuticles.

'The girl was ordered to send the material out, and she refused?'

'That's the way I get it. She let us know in no un- certain terms that she wanted out herself; that is, once she had it in her hands. Can't blame her, I suppose. If it's half as important as I've been led to believe, all hell will break loose down there once it's found to be gone. Can't imagine why it couldn't have been microed.' He watched Guerin closely for his response and asked: 'You know what's in those papers?'

'No idea. And if I follow orders I never will.'

'Funny business.'

Guerin could tell he was not entirely believed. He asked, 'What's the procedure now?'

The resident went back to the papers on his desk. 'You'll

55

go in from Manna Key, shortest run we've got these days. Used to be I'd have a dozen choices, but not nowadays. Small boat but first class. I gave you the best, those were my instructions. Here's your operational sheet.' He handed over a sheaf of papers. 'Ever been on Manna?'

'I've been out to the transmitter on Swan.'

'Same thing, a Godforsaken, barren pile of calcified bird shit. Take something to read.'

'How secure is Manna—what about pursuit or counter action of some kind?'

'We keep a dozen boys on the island, but it's far enough out and tied in close enough with Naval Air so you don't have to worry.' He lit up a Cuban cigarette after offering one to Guerin, and almost disappeared behind a cloud of evil black smoke. 'It's what's called going native, I guess.' He lay back in the chair momentarily and swivelled back and forth. 'Look, I have no info that indicates the Reds are wise, see? Neither does Virgil—I just talked to him this morning—or any of the other residents around the area. God knows, we've got an army of them. But what I wanted to say was there's no reason why it shouldn't go like clockwork. Just the same, I've made the whole operation as tight as I know how. None of the locals know anything about it. It's planned with a four man team, including yourself, coming from around the compass and with no foreknowledge beyond their immediate concerns. You'll go to Manna tomorrow, the twenty-first, the rest of the team to assemble on the twenty-second, Thursday, and you'll all make your run the following day. You should be back here for trans-shipment with the goods by Sunday or Monday. No sweat, no strain.'

'Isn't it always that way?'

Middlebrook laughed a little too enthusiastically. 'No, not around here.'

'What you're telling me is you're a little spooked about this particular operation.'

'Well, yes, I guess I am. But I don't know why. It's just that the avalanche of memorandum on this from topside, it's . . . unusual. Everything about it's so damned imperative you'd think we were knocking over El Maximo Uno himself. Take-outs are a dime a dozen, for Christ's sake. And of course Estrellita going sour on us. She's hiding out in the landing zone—that's always dangerous. I don't know why I'm giving you all this grief, though.'

'I wouldn't like it if you didn't,' Guerin told him bluntly, looking straight into the man's eyes.

Middlebrook read it and decided to respect the innocent-looking but oddly cold young man sitting opposite him. 'I also get a vague feeling of uneasiness or dissatisfaction coming off you, Mercator. Am I right?'

'Reflected heat. If you don't feel right about it, I'd be a fool to think differently.'

'You would be . . . and you're not.' He grunted and finished off his whisky. Guerin, he noted, pushed his aside half-finished in what seemed to him to have been a deliberate gesture. 'Anyway, I've told you what's appropriate and there's nothing else. My secretary will give you your accommodations—not very fancy, I'm afraid—and a schedule to get you to Manna. I'm afraid since it's clandestine, you'll have to go through a lot of ridiculous crap to get down there. I fought against it but as usual LW-3 won. They seem to feel that if anything is simple and direct it's a threat to their job security.' He had assembled the packets of papers on his desk and handed them over. 'Oh, and you'll need expenses—about five thousand—it's all in the packet there but I suggest that you get over this afternoon before the banks close.'

They shook hands but the resident remained seated behind the desk, smiling now. It was like the service, Guerin thought to himself, or any other institution where some men sat in safe places and told others how to risk their lives with a maximum of efficiency and a minimum of cost accrued, the moral disease that wastes to fat. At the door he turned and asked, 'Do you want to talk to the girl before I take her home?'

Middlebrook's expression turned sour, then hard. 'If you just knew what that bitch had caused us—waste her for all I care.' Just as quickly, he relaxed. 'The main thing is, don't leave her there alive. It isn't much of a component, but it's all I have.'

'I have no intention of doing either,' Guerin said as he went, leaving the door open behind him. Middlebrook got up and shut it. There was a phone call coming in and he had done all he could for Mercator; there was other work to do if the world was going to be saved.

Guerin went directly to The National Bank of Miami in the financial district. He filled out a withdrawal form for a special savings account and wrote a set of numbers across the top. At the 'New Accounts' window it was taken by a Vice President who looked him up and down quickly but thoroughly as if he were some rare species of fauna, and then disappeared for ten minutes. When he returned he had almost five thousand American dollars in denominations of less than a hundred and some Cuban pesos in a bulging manilla envelope. It was intended for day to day expenses as well as a sum to be taken ashore on the mission for purposes of bribery, if that be necessary. Guerin could not help smiling at the man's pained expression as he handed it over—he understood how the sense of orderliness required for a successful banking career could rub up against the casual handing over of clandestine monies on the basis of seven numbers written on a piece of paper by a stranger who did not talk.

Later, he roamed through an evening in the barrio. It was a little more risky, certainly, than if he had spent it in Miami Beach, where it could be assumed there were very few members of his own profession on either side to be found, but enough of his life had been constrictedly middle class to give him a taste for exotica, however mild. The food in Cuba, he remembered, had always been terrible, but here it was translated into something closer to Creole and Mexican. After dinner he went from bar to bar, mostly for the music; he was fond of jazz and had always liked what Cubans brought to it. What he found were jukeboxes. The general impoverishment of the exiles was reflected in everything, even music, and gradually the sea of long or angry faces put a pall on the evening. It would have helped had he been free to accept conversation when it was offered.

Slightly drunk, but mostly because he was unwilling to give up on his romantic nostalgia, he picked up a Cuban prostitute on a street corner about midnight and went with her to her apartment. She was thin and sullen, but pretty, and he was lonely enough to go through with it even after she had begun to annoy him.

'What do you do? What is your job?' she asked in Spanish. They were walking down a dank and shabby side-street close to downtown, where the refuse was piled high on the pavement and the salt-sea humidity made an aura around the street lamps, turning the lights slightly green. At first he pretended not to hear and simply shrugged. Too many lies lately.

'I asked you a question,' she persisted, managing to sound critical and dissatisfied with him at the same time that she coiled a professionally feverish hand around his waist and their hips brushed at every step. 'How do you make your living?'

He assumed she thought it was his Spanish which was at fault. 'I understand you, but I'd rather not say, if you don't mind.'

'Why not? You know what I do, why shouldn't I know about you?'

He hoped she was being ironic but a glance at her face

dispelled that hope. 'Because I think it's none of your business.' Jesus, he thought to himself, browbeating a whore! His cover, as verified by the hotel register, was that of an architect—something he had studied briefly in college at his parents' behest—and it would have been so easy to tell the girl that.

'You're rude and mean, like all Anglos,' she said without withdrawing her arm, although there was no mistaking genuine bitterness.

'I'm sorry, let's drop it. Where do you live, for God's sake?' She pointed vaguely up the street. Her failure to invoke the whore's richer invective when she was mad at him, along with her accent, confirmed what he had suspected, that she was originally from the Havana Middle Class. As much to change the subject as anything, he asked her, 'Why did you leave Cuba? I mean, if you hate it here.'

'Why do you think I would leave?' she replied, pouting again. 'Stay and be raped or tortured or killed by the communists?'

'It wasn't like that.'

'Oh? How do you know? Priests ... nuns ... anyone they didn't like.' She raised her voice: 'A pack of filthy atheistic scum!'

Guerin laughed in spite of himself and placed his hand gently over her mouth. 'Where's your sense of propriety?'

When she worked free from his hand she began to rail at length about American abandonment of the exile cause. Her mother and father had gone to Chicago to look for work, and her two brothers to New York. She would not go, she said, she would wait here until Cuba was free. 'Good luck,' Guerin told her.

They entered a cheerless little one-room apartment further subdivided by a series of patched sheets and blankets strung on clothes lines. The girl went directly to a phonograph on the bedside table and started an ancient and very scratched mambo record spinning. It struck Guerin as peculiar and he assumed it was some sort of compulsion, which he was more than willing to allow for in an amateur prostitute, but he objected when she, not satisfied with its considerable volume, turned it up. 'If you want me,' she told him imperiously, 'you will have to accept the conditions.' Oh, God, he thought, save me from amateurs of all kinds. And yet he was too Anglo-Saxon, too guilty, to do anything *but* accept them.

Fortunately for his mood, she wanted sound but not sight, and turned off the light by unscrewing the single bulb in the ceiling. Guerin watched her silhouette undress with singular unresponsiveness, though he still hoped for the arrival of sufficient desire in time to make the effort and risk remotely worth the game. Should he touch her before she went any further, should he try to establish some warmth, however ersatz, if only to make the lies easier for both of them? He had been with prostitutes before but he had never had to ask these questions of himself. Traces of sweat appeared on his face and he wiped it away with two fingers, reassuring himself that it would never be noticed in the ensuing combat in the dark, presuming he could bring himself to the battlefield. It was not strictly a sexual fear he was grappling with, but the thought that the inability to share experience with others or even to feel anything at all, which had begun as a cerebral awareness had crept down into the most primary part of him. At last, when she began to undress in the ancient perfunctory way, something fundamental reasserted itself and all the parts worked again. By the time he entered her, he was reassuring himself, rationalizing, that the problem was nothing more than too many pills between assignments.

They made furtive and mechanical love on a steel cot covered by a Seminole Indian blanket. When it was over Guerin faced up to what he had suspected from the beginning: 'There's someone behind that sheet hanging over there.'

'Yes,' she admitted, while dressing to go back to work, 'that's my grandmother. It doesn't matter any more. Besides, her hearing is rather poor.'

The old lady coughed above the wheeze of the expiring phonograph, and Guerin, sweating profusely now, groaned as if in reply. Quickly, he paid the agreed fifteen dollars and then added ten more for no defensible reason. The girl was not very grateful and that made him feel better. He finished dressing and went outside without saying goodbye. He had even managed not to know her name, and the universality in that consoled him somehow, too.

It was while turning off Flower Street on to Biscayne in search of another universal remedy, a cold beer and strong cigar, that Guerin realized he had a tag. How long it had been there he could not say for certain, because even the moment of recognition was difficult to pinpoint. It was always that way, some instinct, a sense that the rhythm around you had changed. He did the usual things, stopping to glance back casually, once trying to use the strong reflection in a blackened window. The man would know what he was doing, but no matter, and the casualness was simply routine precaution in that sudden movement might be interpreted as a threat and thus precipitate violence. So it was all as stylized as some absurd ballet; Guerin would walk and stop, the tag would do the same. Guerin looked back again, the man, following again, found something noncommittal to do. He had deliberately left his hand gun in the hotel room, but half-regretted it now.

Guerin walked a little faster and the man hung on. He was sweating again and it had reached all the way through to spot his seersucker jacket. Ridiculous to think of a thing like that, yet it galled him. The truth was, he was angry with himself; he had been brazenly careless and undisciplined about the girl, and now here he was being caught up for it within moments after the lapse. He ran the last two or three assignments through his memory bank to see whether or not they bore a residual potential for violence, but could think of nothing; it had to be this one, this one that might look relatively routine but had somehow been wrong from the beginning.

The tag was a Cuban, or at least a Latin. Well dressed, coat and tie, and in the present context that was not particularly good news; it meant he was probably from the Firm—or one of the exile groups, all of whom had some tenuous relationship with the Firm. The Hostiles in this theatre seemed to consider ties hopelessly bourgeois, even in secret agents. For what possible reason could anyone in the Firm want him trailed at this point?

Unless, of course, there was something to Sandy's bizarre ramblings. The sidewalks were empty but a number of cars still rushed through the broad, palm-lined boulevard; Guerin tried to use them to shake his tag by dashing across suddenly, timing his break to give him the optimum escape time. It did not work, the man was good at what he did and was still with him when he reached his hotel. There was nothing else for it but to go up to his room and try to sleep, although not before placing a chair firmly against the door, a vase balanced delicately beside the window jamb and a spread of crumpled newspapers around his bed. Tomorrow he would be at a secret base in the Caribbean, the tag could not follow him there. If only he would be a good guy or a bad operative and not report the whore, but that was altogether too much to hope for. Guerin, in his place, would certainly have told.

6

He arose earlier than necessary by half an hour and exercised and cold-showered to put himself ahead of the day. He failed to remember the whore until he had entered the shower, a natural place for it, and then found himself surprisingly lighthearted, even at the prospect that he might have caught something from her. While he scrubbed away, he made up headlines concerning that event for the yellow press, which to his mind was most of the press, or imagined explaining to a congressional or departmental committee how he had given her vagina a routine security check before entering, but something had gone wrong. 'Of course I knew she was a Troskyite with Anarcho-syndicalist tendencies, Senator, but we always stress daring and resolution at the Firm. Our manual borrows heavily from the Israeli army—"The route to safety is the closest way to the enemy hill".'

He went out and walked hard for twenty minutes before breakfast, lured back into the barrio by the dark smells of *café con leche* until he found a Mexican restaurant where he could start the day with *huevos rancheros* and a bottle of Dos Ecces. He had slept well too, as he usually did when there was the possibility of risk.

It took only a moment to pack. Now he removed the Walther P-38 pistol from his suitcase and placed it inside his coat, for they would be leaving the cities behind and it made more sense to carry a weapon. The driver who picked him up at his hotel was a Cuban, despite Middle-brook's assurances that 'they' had been categorically excluded. But this one turned out atypically to be so taciturn he said almost nothing for the whole trip, which carried Guerin out from Miami along the Tamiami Trail to a primitive private airport deep in the Everglades. From there he was flown in an unmarked civilian plane piloted by a young, clean-cut Anglo with a military haircut and a Southern accent. Under complete radio silence they crossed out over the Caribbean on a slightly westerly course.

Guerin, curious, asked him: 'Where are we headed?' He found he had to shout above the motor and repeat everything he said, possibly because the man did not want to hear him.

'Corn Islands, sir.'

'What the hell for?'

'Orders, sir.'

'I know that, for Christ's sake, but why do they include taking me all the hell the way to Nicaragua?'

The pilot seemed not at all offended and answered matter-of-factly, 'You'll have to go in by seaplane. Besides, we always approach the forward bases from some direction other than the United States. It's deception.'

'Of course. In case there are any Reuters correspondents cruising around down there in rowboats, they won't get the idea we've got any interest in Cuba. The court of world opinion, is that it?'

'I don't get you, sir?'

'Where did you learn all that "sir" business?'

'Alabama Air National Guard, sir.'

'I should have known,' Guerin murmured, as he sat back to try and study his operational papers. Sea and sky were beautiful, it would be difficult to concentrate. The young pilot did not count.

It took nine hours to get to Manna Key. Very much what Guerin had expected in the way of a facility—half a dozen buildings of the plantation variety, a few too many, actually, for the agricultural potential suggested by

65

the island itself. The seaplane landed expertly in a tiny lagoon and he rowed ashore in a dingy to be met by a gaunt, middle-aged man named Burke, who described himself as the 'station manager'. The way the skin was etched tightly across prominent bones, pink on top and sallow under the stubble of beard, the dark circled eyes, gave Guerin an impression of 'American Gothic'. Burke was decorous, almost formal in his greeting, but he made no effort to introduce the new arrival to the staff. He was told there were nine of them currently; seven Americans, an Australian and a Cuban, and he saw maybe half a dozen in the course of his brief stay. They were friendly and would wave in passing, but that was as close as they would get to communicating with him. He understood. Probably the majority of men who went out from this place never returned.

He rested in the room they gave him and then had dinner alone with Burke, save for a single, silent orderly, the Cuban. Caste, Guerin thought to himself, even here. Well, why not here especially? The older man was easy but dull; he talked mostly of growing up in Washington state and how he would retire there someday and grow enormous organically created apples in great quantity and become rich in a country God was still preserving for those who could appreciate it. They touched briefly on politics, and Guerin, who was not political himself except in an academic sense, gathered that his host considered Herbert Hoover to be the first in a long uninterrupted line of flaming radicals who have dominated the United States ever since. So much for politics—there were plenty of these in the Firm and it was best to ignore them. Still, the man offered him a half bottle of excellent brandy before retiring. 'Not much to do here, we go to bed early after awhile. You'll see, it's the rhythm of the place. Nature demands it of you.'

Guerin took the bottle with him while he wandered

the perimeter of the island to work up a fatigue. A cloud-less sky was spread with stars in such profusion it made him giddy. The moon lay slantwise just above a gentle tropical surf, and all of it together so affected him with memories and sensations he knew he would probably not sleep at all. What had Middlebrook said, 'A pile of calcified bird shit?' He threw the emptied brandy bottle out over the incoming waves, where it made a mysterious splash and started on its way to the world's end.

In the morning there was a boat in the lagoon, a small cabin cruiser which tried, but could not quite hide its souped-up motor and rakish intent. Guerin saw it from the window and it caused him to dress quickly, putting on his whites and sneakers, in order to be there when the dinghy came ashore. It was important that even in little things these men should feel that he cared. Burke was already waiting at the landing point when he got there.

Guerin hailed him on the way down. 'Those ought to be mine.'

'They are,' the older man assured him. 'Nice looking boat. New one. Never used it here before, anyway.'

'You run many missions in and out of here?' Guerin asked, as he came abreast.

'A lot more go out than come in.'

To Guerin the place seemed ridiculously open and ex-posed and he had even heard that a reporter had once been out here, as well as a retired couple who landed accidentally in the course of a stumbling trip around the world. The Cubans could scarcely be unaware of its exis-tence, any more than they could of Swan. He glanced out at the boat to estimate its height above the water, and was reassured that Cuban radar, which certainly had the range, would have trouble getting a fix nevertheless.

'Regular United Nations,' Burke commented as the

dinghy drew near shore. He glanced out of the corner of his eye for Guerin's reaction.

They had sent him three men; from here one looked to be a Negro, a tall rangy man built like a basketball player, whose large hands closed over a machine pistol across his lap; another was a little wiry Cuban and he seemed to have the savvy with the boat, probably his captain. The third, scarcely touched yet by the local sun, was contrastingly an Anglo-type behind the requisite dark glasses. All three wore the stripped-down fatigues they would use on the run. When they reached the surf and piled into the water to drag the raft ashore, Burke and Guerin waded out to help.

The 'Anglo' abandoned the dinghy to come ahead, one hand outstretched to Guerin, whisking off his glasses with the other. 'Stephen,' he called, 'we drew one together.'

Guerin accepted the handshake reservedly and his voice was cool and flat when he admonished: 'Mercator.'

Sandy looked a little hurt. 'Fox,' he introduced himself.

On the beach the Cuban said he was 'Blue' and the Negro, who turned out to be an American, was called 'Homer'.

'Why did you bring that ashore?' Guerin asked the Negro, indicating the Schmeisser.

'You never know,' Homer told him, without smiling. 'Besides, it makes me happy.'

Guerin's mouth turned down in a characteristic expression of displeasure. 'It doesn't make me happy, you'll stow it.'

'Yes, sir.'

Guerin realized on the way up to Burke's quarters that he was over-reacting to his surprise and dislike for Sandy's presence on the mission, something that had really shaken him. But he had no intention of backing down on Homer; romantics and sadists, authoritarians and gun-lovers in general would be kept under tight discipline where he had the command. Still, there were very few Negroes in

68

the Firm, so the odds were the man was at least good at what he did.

A subdued, deliberately impersonal lunch was followed by four hours of conference and briefing in a sound-proofed room from which even Burke was excluded. Blue turned out to have been a fisherman who knew the particular stretch of southeast coastline so well Guerin had only to show him the charts. Homer was assigned as weapons man and, inexplicably, had expectation of going ashore.

'No, Fox goes alone. There'll be no need for gunnery ashore. It would only get in the way.'

'Excuse me, sir, but I got my orders to go ashore with Fox.'

Guerin, who was standing at the blackboard, paused to light a small cigar. He needed the moment. Something was distinctly wrong, and it cried out warning in every word Homer uttered.

'Who gave you those orders?'

Homer looked around for a moment, as if to inquire if that was not an incredible question. 'My resident where I was stationed, when he assigned me here.'

'Who?'

'I can't tell you that, obviously.'

The man was dangerously underestimating him, Guerin knew, but he was used to that. He lowered his voice to a near whisper, a technique he had found, oddly enough, effective both with children and people who thought of themselves as very hard. 'You were also told to report to a man named Mercator, who is in command of this operation. I am Mercator, if you didn't know.'

'Look, I told you, I already got—'

Guerin's voice came up slightly as he broke in, each word sharp and clear: 'Then one of two things will happen to you—either I will have you placed under arrest and taken off this island in chains, or I will personally blow your fucking head off, you insubordinate black bastard.'

When, in the silence that followed, Homer failed to leave his chair, Guerin knew he had won. Every word had been calculated, including the racial slur; he was not playing the elegant white liberal if it meant putting himself up as a target for a black fascist executioner. More likely he was intended to kill the girl and leave her behind, for if it was Guerin himself someone wanted eliminated it would not make sense for Homer to put him on edge through naked defiance. They had tried a bluff and lost.

His eyes roamed from one to another of the three faces confronting him. Blue was silent and impassive; he was the most self-contained Cuban Guerin had ever seen, and he had had to fight off the tendency to judge him competent on that alone. Homer stared past him, breathing hardly at all, his face rigid but expressionless, with only the tiny metallic flame lighting the pupils of his eyes to show that he was alive and hating. Fox looked puzzled and embarrassed. Guerin had always thought he lacked the essential hardness for their profession.

The rest of the briefing passed off uneventfully. Guerin was anxious to get through with it for a number of reasons, but principally because it was now less than fourteen hours until they would cast off and it was important he speak to Sandy alone before making certain decisions. Burke came in at the end, apologizing for the interruption, and asked if they would not have dinner with him up at the main bungalow in an hour, and if they minded having seafood, which was more or less staple on this station? Guerin said they would be delighted and asked that now the rest of the component on the island join them.

'You don't know the losses we've suffered in people coming through here,' Burke replied, shaking his head adamantly. 'It's bad for morale and bad for security.'

Guerin acceded. Burke was, after all, resident commander, but personally he felt such policies were wrong, had once even written an article for the 'in house' journal which maintained in effect that security which ended in alienation was no security at all. He dismissed the present meeting by saying that he wanted to talk to Fox alone, since he was the only agent who would set foot on the objective. Then he took his friend out along the shore where even a shotgun mike would be rendered useless by the pounding of the surf.

'Why you, Sandy?' he asked. 'I have to know that.'

'What makes you think I know?'

'Everyone else on this operation seems to have been told all about it.'

'It's like I told you the other night out at the restaurant: I was to report for an overseas assignment the next morning. This was it. By some cockamamie route through, I think it was, New Orleans—they kept the windows masked.'

'Who gave you your orders?'

Sanford paused for maximum effect, then with superb underplaying managed a casual: 'Guy named Hammerle.'

Guerin came close to hating him for it. 'Okay, I'm ready to listen now,' was all he said.

'To what, Stephen?'

Guerin stopped walking and turned to face him angrily. 'For Christ's sake, man, in Washington you were ready to spill your guts, if only I'd let you.'

'That's changed.'

'What's changed? Not for me it hasn't! You told me you'd got mixed up with the factionalism and that you had reason to think your next assignment could be the means by which someone executed you. You knew all about Hammerle and my mission when you had no business to. We've never worked outside together before, it's not coincidence we're together now.'

'It isn't you they want to kill, it's me—I told you that.'

'Look, it's this arrogant hard-nosed spade, isn't it?'

71

Sanford shifted his feet uneasily. 'I don't know, and neither do you. That scene at the briefing ... I just didn't recognize you in it ... I mean the racial business.'

Guerin looked away and up at the stabbing blue sky above the sea, shielding his eyes. He was not naturally a patient man, except by great effort, and sometimes answering the obvious was just too painful. Anyway, it was all going wrong somehow. 'Sandy, on occasion you're just too goddamned Jewish.'

'I don't have much of a sense of humour these days, Stephen.' The tone was grating and sour, as if confirming the words.

Guerin started walking again and the smaller man followed, almost unwillingly. 'I wanted to tighten him up,' he explained. Sandy seemed to accept that.

'It's falling apart, Stephen, the Firm is, why don't you get out?'

'You mean cross over?'

Sanford could not help himself, he laughed. 'Why would you assume automatically I meant defect? There are other ways to live, you know.'

'You're not going in tomorrow night. I am.'

'What?' Sanford's face dropped in disbelief. He looked at Guerin, but his friend was staring off again. 'What the hell does that mean?'

The sun had begun to slip down the sky and they had gone to the water's edge to meet it. Guerin was watching a seagull gliding effortlessly with the trade winds behind it and wondering what prevented him from going the same way. 'It's not,' he spoke up, 'a negotiable decision.'

'That's wrong, I know your orders. You were not to go in. You'd be insubordinate.'

'You know too goddamned much. Listen to me ...' He picked up a piece of coral and used it to scatter some sitting gulls so that he might watch their flight, while Sanford marvelled at the peculiar combination of boyishness and ruthless precision that mingled in him. Guerin went on: 'You know how these things are done. If they intend to kill you, really intend to, it will be on Cuban soil. No court of inquiry there, except Cuban, and they wouldn't care ...'

'You can't scrub the mission because of me, because of a fight you say yourself you're not part of.'

'To hell with you, I'm going in myself for precisely that reason—the mission. Whether or not I'm disobeying orders is really none of your business, *Fox*, I have the authority.'

'Can I go back now?' Sandy asked coldy. 'I want some sack time before dinner.' He added that he had not been sleeping well lately.

Guerin nodded dismissal. Sanford went a little way and then paused. Not quite over his shoulder, he said, 'You know, you were right, I was trying to recruit you the other night.'

'I knew,' Guerin said. He seemed sad.

'It's too late now—I thought you should know that. I owe you that. You were judged too ... professional. If I were you, I'd give some thought to the other side, the Quarry people. You'll need someone, Stephen.'

'Watch the black, Sandy, or he'll blow *your* fucking head off.'

Sanford went up to the central building, his shoulders sloping and head forward against the rising wind. Guerin stayed where he was and watched the gulls.

7

They sailed before dawn the next day, making such good time in spite of a choppy sea that it would become necessary to do some circling before beginning the final run under cover of darkness that night. The boat was fine, Guerin noted with satisfaction, fast enough under its deceptively tacky appearance to outrun anything except, perhaps, one of the Russian-made MTBs. Of course if the planes got on you in daylight it was all over anyway. Blue proved to be the first-rate captain he had looked, and drove the boat as though its hard metal was an extension of his small brown body.

About nightfall, when they ceased evasive manoeuvres and began their direct approach to the coast, Guerin came next to Blue at the wheel and asked him about himself in Spanish. 'Are you from one of the exile groups?'

'No, sir, I was living in Jamaica for a long time.'

'How old are you?'

'About fifty years.'

'Why do you do this?' The little man shrugged his indifference with embarrassment. Guerin liked him, liked his style. 'It's very dangerous,' he pressed.

'That's all right, they pay me well for it.'

'No patriotism? No politics?'

The Cuban shrugged again. 'I am always on the water, doing something. How can you have politics in a boat with two or three people. Anyway, Cuba has always had bad governments, why should this one be different?'

'This one is supposed to be good for the poor people. Especially fishermen, people like yourself.'

If Blue had any idea that Guerin was trying to entrap him, he did not show it. He said matter-of-factly, 'I am from Jamaica.'

'I like the way you handle the boat. You know your job well.'

'How do you know that? Wait until I get you in, and maybe out again.'

Guerin smiled. 'I'll come back and we'll go fishing together. You know, after all this is over.'

The Cuban spat into the wind. 'Let's see if you are alive the day after tomorrow.'

'I'll be back, and I'm bringing you a pretty Habanera.'

'I'm too old.'

The candied slice of moon Guerin had admired the night before was now obscured by general cloudiness true to the prediction of the Naval Meteorological Department. As he climbed down from the conning position, Guerin got a glimpse of Homer working to mount a 20-mm Swedish Bofors gun on the bow. On the stern he had already laid out hand guns and clips, two Schmeissers and a Belgian rifle with an infra-red sniper scope attachment. Beside them was the medical kit and a canteen. Homer was obviously thorough, and tonight that pleased even Guerin.

At eleven-twenty Blue announced that the coast was within sight and they turned east slightly to line up with the landing point. Guerin went in to the cabin to begin a check on his not very extensive equipment with Sandy's help. The sea was building up and spray beginning to come into the cockpit, so he was grateful for the pea-jacket which contained most of the things he had to carry. Probably later he would hate it for its bulk and weight, particularly if there was any trouble.

'Why did you do that?' Sandy asked him, when he leaned out and threw the cyanide ampules over the side. He seemed a little shocked.

'Don't you always?'

'No, of course not.'

'Well, I'll admit there are times when I've taken them seriously, but, face it Sandy, there's no justification for them here when it's common knowledge we infiltrate the island regularly. And I don't know anything of importance they don't already know. Besides, the Cubans won't use torture anyway, not the real thing—a matter of revolutionary pride with them.'

'I've heard that crap, too, but I don't believe it. And there's always drugs.'

Guerin showed the automatic in the pocket of his jacket. 'There's always this ... whatever.'

'That's not enough either,' Sandy said doggedly. 'I know how you are about guns, but it's indefensible—you ought to take one of the Schmeissers, the one with the silencer. Particularly if you've come around on this business with the "Element".' He glanced at Homer. 'If it's a trap of some kind you'll damn well need the firepower.'

Homer's voice came on the wind from the front: 'There it is! Punta Ladrilla.'

The two agents rushed out to look, leaning over the side paralleling the coast. There, far away, was a tiny wink of flame which acted both as a beacon and a diversionary signal fire between them and the nearest Cuban naval patrol base. Blue turned the engine up to full power, anxious to leave it behind as quickly as possible.

'I have to get on the radio,' Sandy told him, and then Guerin was alone on deck. Always the best way to be, he thought, before you put your life on the line.

He disciplined himself by the clock before beginning a clandestine mission, counting off even that time allowed for nostalgia—the children got fifteen minutes. The Walther was oiled and placed in a watertight plastic wrapper before being returned to the pocket of his peajacket. Otherwise, he took a Swiss army knife, some chocolate, two hundred dollars worth of Cuban pesos in addition to his American money, a flashlight with ultraviolet filter for signalling and a small medical kit.

'I've got it!' Sandy cried from inside the cabin, turning up the radio so the high-pitched whine of the approach signal could be heard by everyone above the building roar of the wind and waves. The signal informed them that it was safe to land, but they knew there would be no further messages coming over so Sandy turned off the radio and came up to help his friend. Already, brooding stands of giant palm could be seen ahead whenever the boat crested a wave and the pale fickle moonlight allowed.

'Stephen, it should be me.'

Guerin, distracted, running the last minute check on his person, answered irritably: 'For Christ's sake, can the first name business, would you. You know better.'

'Sorry.'

'So am I, sorry I had to have lunch in the commissary last Tuesday.' He felt the pitch under the boat change from deep water to shoreline swells. The flash of the surf was visible directly ahead. He heard Blue and Homer shouting back and forth up front but he could not understand what they were saying. His stomach was knotting up but he felt good in spite of that—the adrenals were pumping furiously.

Sandy was rambling on about his own concerns: 'You'll have to open your eyes some day. If you don't join one party or the other pretty soon they'll ease you out, or maybe worse. Both sides hate neutrals now ... the thing is polarizing.'

Guerin was leaning out, straining to see the shore. 'You told me it was too late to join the "Bourse", they wouldn't have me now.'

'If I get back maybe I can change it. I'm only a functionary but—'

He was interrupted by the sudden appearance of Homer, who leaped down into the cockpit from the top of the cabin in a single jarring move which sent Guerin's hand part-way to his jacket pocket.

'Blue says he saw a light to the west and behind us. I think I saw it too. There's nobody out here at this hour except patrol boats.'

Guerin ran it through for a few seconds, then cast a

glance at the rapidly closing beach. 'We're this near, we'll go in. Blue knows the procedures if you're jumped or I don't come back in time. He'll take you out behind Los Jardines de la Reina.'

Homer nodded and reached for a machine pistol. He handed it to Sandy, taking the other one himself. 'What we haven't seen,' he commented casually, 'is the signal light from the beach. Blue's sure he knows the exact spot though, so it looks like you just got to trust him.'

'I do.' Guerin met Homer's smile with one of his own, equally malevolent.

Sandy looked on with large solemn eyes and said nothing. Homer turned his smile to him for an instant before going back to his gun position on the bow. When he was gone, Guerin climbed onto the railing, clinging tightly to keep from being bucked off by the surf, and saw for himself that there was no beacon light anywhere up or down the coast. Sandy put his machine pistol at a ready position and settled down along the bulkhead on the side Blue was swinging into shore. Guerin, glancing at him, thought he looked like a toy sailor in his denims.

Indicating the gun, he called out to him softly: 'You keep that in your hands till I get back.'

'Good luck, Mercator,' came the whispered response, although its imperativeness was the only thing that survived transmission now that the boat was churning sand in its struggle to survive the angry water.

Blue yelled, 'Okay, pronto!' and Guerin leaped, his heart in his throat lest the opaque snarling eddies beneath his feet held some trap, a hole that could topple him into the ebbtide or a projection sharp enough to pierce the sole of his sneakers. But he was lucky; if it was not sand it was certainly finely ground coral—the sheer malignancy of the surf here would account for that.

Blue was anxious to get the boat off the beach and began backing and filling before Guerin was clear, almost taking him out with it. A good-sized wave caught him flat when the water was only waist deep but he was still leaning forward to escape the propellers of the boat; he went over into a nightmare of suffocating black water, thrashing about like a madman to regain his feet. In the shock of going down he had sucked in and now his mouth and throat and lungs were bubbling and boiling, shrieking for air. Only the happenstance timing of the waves saved him because the next one was relatively small; had it been as powerful as the first he would have died.

He staggered ashore and fell down heavily on the beach. Thoughts of security, of the man who should have been there to meet him, to help him, were put aside while he vomited back the sea and some of his fear. He was not that kind of a brave man. Twisting around to look at what he had escaped from, he found the boat, running without lights, had already disappeared into what was for him, lying nearly prone, a white wallscreen of foam and great lurching waves. There was no one else on the beach and the only land sound came from the nagging of the wind. He sprang up immediately and faded into the scrub palm and high grass that lay behind the beach, where he could remain relatively hidden while he sorted out his dilemma.

He had three hours before they would return for him; that is, if the weather allowed. Should anything at all go wrong, the boat would come back to this same place in twenty-four hours, but that would end their obligation to him; after that he was entirely on his own. Of course another mission might be organized later to take him out, should he by some miracle survive. So he had two apparent choices, either to wait for daylight and try to seek out members of the underground himself, which would be extremely risky since he had only a paper knowledge of where they were or the geography of the place where he now was, or he could search the beach in the dark and hope that the prospect of a storm would keep it bereft of patrols. In the end, he decided against either one and remained where he was, hoping that Blue's navigational skill was as good as he boasted and that the little Cuban had put him down exactly where he ought to be.

The pallid moon reappeared long enough to allow him to examine his equipment for water damage. There was none. He flipped back the lid on his watch and the luminous dial showed how accurate the timing had been on their side—it was now eighteen minutes past the moment of rendez-vous. A lot of good that would do him if the underground were operating at their usual level of efficiency. Guerin sat back against a rock, smiling icily at the thought that right now two brave, committed 'gusanos' were probably arguing over whether he was landing on the north or south coast, on Tuesday or Thursday.

He shivered as the wind poured in on his soggy clothes, drying them but chilling him badly enough to make him reconsider his decision to stay put and wait. There were, after all, two solid bits of evidence that indicated he was being sought by the underground, first the diversionary fire up the coast, and then the radio signal just before they beached. But he had no way of knowing where the transmitter was placed, and therefore whether or not there was close and accurate co-ordination between the different elements which had separate functions. He had been told there was, and indeed this was one of the last areas remaining in Cuba where conditions were favourable to take-out operations; it was primitive, lightly populated and there were over a dozen locals who were actively engaged against the regime. But also an 'apparat', as the Hostiles called them, could be swamped overnight, could be broken by a single mistake or a weak member, and its personnel replaced by provocateurs. And as for the fire down the coast, that was double-edged, too, the sort of amateur play that worked if the enemy was present in numbers and you accomplished your business quickly and efficiently;

when things went wrong it had the negative effect of bringing him into the neighbourhood and telling him something was up.

Guerin moved out, keeping close to the beach but clear of its whiteness. The rustle of scrub, whenever he brushed up against it, counted for nothing because of the wind. He went west at first, but that soon turned into swamp down almost to the water's edge, and he knew the village of Tunas de Zaza was not very far in that direction anyway, so he reversed himself and worked his way about a quarter of a mile east of his original landing place. At a bend in the coast it seemed prudent to cut across the base of an outcropping that was flat and exposed at its tip. If he had not done so he would never have found his contact.

8

Amazingly, it was the dull, filtered red circle of light from the man's flashlight that showed him first. Evidently, Guerin reasoned afterwards, he had been using it in his futile attempt to locate their boat and had forgotten to turn it off, so that when he headed inland again it bobbled in front of him like the announcement that a locomotive was coming. But that thinking came later and at the moment of intercept it almost cost the man his life, for Guerin had his automatic, safety off, aimed at his thorax from a prone position almost instantly. The man may have seen him go down or in some way sensed the movement because he stopped, and when the low-pitched cry came, 'Alto!' he remained frozen where he was. If he had moved for any reason at all, Guerin had already determined, in that moment between standing and violently stretching out on the ground, to kill him.

'Now come towards me slowly,' he told the man in Spanish, and the man did. Guerin rose cautiously to a kneeling position, maintaining the proper fulcrum for his weapon, and asked: 'What makes Cuban cigars?' A high-pitched voice, either frightened or broken by the wind, came back with a quavering but correct counter-sign: 'Love and Cuban tobacco.' They were passwords that had caused Guerin, when he had found them in the file on the plane down to Manna Key, to wonder if some exiled advertising man had not found a niche for himself in the Firm, but then all passwords were somehow fatuous, even the simplest.

For the next twenty minutes he followed the man through heavy undergrowth over periodically swampy terrain. He never discovered his guide's name, never in fact got a good look at him, and knew nothing about him at all except that he seemed rather old and his clothes were ragged. A peasant or possibly a fisherman from the way he carried himself. Guerin did not reprove him for his carelessness with the signal light; since no one back at the Firm believed these people could endure as an organization anyway, there would simply be no point to it.

They came to a coastal road and paused behind a cypress while his guide tilted his head to the wind and then the ground, like a Plains Indian sniffing out the cavalry. For Guerin's part, he could see that there was nothing coming from either direction and the road was such that at night a vehicle could be spotted long before anyone in it could get a look at them. Still, he did not like the idea of a road bisecting his escape route. He jumped up and ran across the few yards of pavement without waiting for the old man, anxious to reach his objective and get out again in time for the return of the boat.

The old man caught up with him, puffing but showing no indication of disapproval, and took him to a peasant's hut separated from the road only by a clump of Australian pines. He knocked in some sort of mysterioso way and then disappeared with a stealthiness which Guerin found time to admire, in one so old, before the door was yanked open and he was urged inside. A young boy, maybe fourteen or fifteen, was behind the door and shut it just as quickly after him. Bad practice, sign of a crumbling network when they recruit babies. Across the room a middle-aged man, heavy-lidded and saturnine-looking, sat at a rude table. Both wore soiled white shirts and pants and were barefoot. Neither was armed and they looked at Guerin, who was still carrying the automatic against his thigh, reproach-fully. He put on the safety and slipped it back into his jacket pocket; if this was a trap he was already too deeply into it to hope that a pistol could get him out.

The boy retired to a corner of the room where he had an obviously familiar chair surrounded by his few belong-ings. Both men stared and said nothing. A single oil lamp burned on the table.

'You are not electrified here?' Guerin opened casually in Spanish.

'Not yet,' the man answered.

The boy spoke up eagerly to assure the Yankee stranger that it was right around the corner, a matter of months according to the District Committee for the Revolution.

The man at the table gave him a disapproving look. He turned to Guerin and told him: 'When it does, the revolu-tion will be over here.'

'Which revolution?'

'The Christian revolution.'

'Oh, I see, the counter-revolution. Why will it be over?'

'Because the people around here, the rural people, are animals, prepared to sell their spiritual birthright, the sacred ethos of the Cuban nation, for the material gains offered them by those criminals in Havana.'

Nothing sluggish about him now from the neck up; his face was animated, the eyes opened and began to glisten.

They must have to keep this one well out of sight, Guerin thought. Even physically no one would mistake him for a peasant with those butterfly hands and ivory feet that looked naked out of shoes. Disguise was rarely successful across ethnic or class lines, he knew. The boy was a different matter, despite the fact that he somehow looked like the older man and had momentarily fooled Guerin into thinking they must be related, it was clear now from his calloused stumpiness that he was local, brought into the underground by religion or intimidation or even money, or the simple prospect of excitement. He looked back and forth between the two men with a puzzled expression, not sure whether he had the right to welcome electrification or not. The Yankee smiled at him and he seemed reassured.

Guerin felt he had stretched his own needs to meet the requirements of Latin courtesy beyond the point of logic. True, he had not commented upon the climate, had not even learned the name of his host, but there was the business, he reminded them, of the girl. 'You are taking her out?' the man asked. Guerin nodded, wondering how much he knew.

The man stood and pounded rhythmically on the back wall, the same mumbo-jumbo knock the old man had used to get Guerin admitted. Then he sagged, as if exhausted by the effort, and turned to his Yankee guest. 'Not everybody is so fortunate as to leave this communist outhouse.'

'Why don't you go?'

The Cuban gave an eyebrow-lifting tour-de-force of sarcasm. 'Have I your permission?'

'I'm here to take out the girl. That's the only one I can take out. As for permission, I don't know what you're talking about.'

Where the hell was the girl? All he could think of was that the pounding on the wall had simply been to alert a runner who would then go and get her from another

84

location. He glanced at his watch and then took a listen to the wind. It was his impression that it had not built up any more in the last half hour, and it might yet be that Blue had been right when he told him it would not turn into a major storm. Still, time was problem enough.

The man went on with his complaint while the peasant boy sat in the corner amidst his handmade fishing equipment and Mickey Mouse comic books. 'You know very well it is your people who keep me here. I was told that if I came down to live among these wretched peasants I would be brought out—I was a lawyer with many international contacts—but it is three months now. I do everything I am told, like this tonight, and I suspect I am being given the more dangerous jobs, because they hate me and think I am good only as a sacrificial goat. They know the boy won't be shot, he's too young ...'

Guerin glanced out of the corner of his eye and noted the boy had rolled a crude cigarette and was lighting it up luxuriously—that cheered him. At this point the girl came in. She was rather tall and moved like a dancer, he thought, without making a sound, but at the same time directly and without show. Wilful, a little aggressive, her walk announced. She was wearing slacks and a light sweater and canvas sneakers of a variety worn by chic young American matrons for sport and play, a fact he did not notice at the time, but something that should have struck him as odd considering the limitations on footwear in Havana and the length of time she had been there. The main thing was that she had arrived and he could see his way out.

They introduced themselves to each other, Guerin calling himself Mercator and the girl saying her name was Julia Fernandez. Insensibly, he insisted she tell him her code name.

'I thought I was through with all that nonsense,' she told him, with a kind of arch smile, evidently feeling out his attitudes since she would need him to effect her escape. Guerin simply waited, and finally she told him: 'Estrellita'. Switching to English, she asked, 'A little corny, don't you think?' Guerin remembered how much of her life had been lived on the underbelly of New York.

'I have to talk to you alone,' he insisted, but in Spanish so as not to affront the others.

'Why can't we do that on the boat?'

'Because I want to talk to you *before* we take you out.'

'Oh, I see. Well, there's nowhere, unless you want to go down and sit in the swamp.' She indicated the lawyer, and Guerin recognized that there would be no love lost between them. 'He never goes out except to the toilet. And he's just gone, too, so I don't think it would pay us to wait.'

Guerin turned to the lawyer. 'I'm sorry, but I must be alone with her when we talk.' The man did not seem to know whether he would comply or not, so Guerin added, 'Take him with you,' pointing to the boy in the corner.

'We could just talk in English, he doesn't speak much,' the girl said.

'Come back in ten minutes, but no sooner,' Guerin pressed the lawyer. Casually he slipped his hand into the pocket that contained the automatic, not that he had any intention of really threatening him with it, but, guessing the man he was dealing with was a total stranger to real violence, simply as an expediter. The man went. 'Go on, chico, you too,' Guerin waved for the boy to follow, and he went with a grin, possibly because of the way the Yankee had treated the windbag.

Now it was Estrellita's turn to prove herself ... 'Julia!' she haggled, 'I'm not even going to talk to you unless you call me by my right name—it's a pretty one, don't you think? Julia?'

'Let's just put that kind of crap to one side now, will

you ... Maybe you've been in Cuba too long.'

The girl smiled pleasantly. 'We agree on that.'

'Where the hell is the file? Why don't you have it with you?'

'Are you here to get me out or aren't you?'

'Where are the papers you stole from the Ministry of the Interior on July twenty-sixth?'

'I asked *you* a question.'

'We never buy on time, you should know that. When I've seen the file and verified its authenticity according to certain criteria I've been given, then we go. You can be in Miami in forty-eight hours.'

The wind rattled the hut to its sickly foundations and crept through the walls to bat about the flame in the oil lamp, weaving disjointed patterns across the composure of Julia's slightly oriental face. She went and sat on the single wooden bed in the room and stared at him, still smiling confidently. Guerin's mind left the track for a moment to make the obvious connection of a handsome woman and a bed, and he was disconcerted by its obviousness. He did not like to think of himself as that simple.

'I don't have it,' she said matter-of-factly.

'Why not? Where is it?' He had known from the beginning, of course, that something was wrong, and now he was going to play it as detached as she was.

'Because I think if you have it you won't take me out.'

'We have to honour our word like anyone else, and for the same reasons.'

'You honour your word when people would know if you didn't. But this is Cuba, not Berlin, and you can get away with anything here. Besides, I'm only a stringer.'

Guerin exhaled heavily and stood up, as if to go. Glancing at his watch he said, 'I have just over half an hour to get back and the surf is probably worse than when I came in, and getting rougher. To tell you the truth, it scares the hell out of me, but I'd rather take my chances with it than the G-2.'

'Do you have an American cigarette before you go?'

Guerin smoked cigars but he carried cigarettes for others when he went to places where they were unobtainable. He crossed and gave her one, staying to light it. Obviously he was not going. 'You've blown your cover. You're not in a position to bargain.'

'Ah,' she said, 'now you are beginning to behave the way I expected.'

'Nobody asked you to blow it, in fact you were ordered not to. Now you're compounding your disobedience and accusing us of bad faith in addition.'

'It's funny,' she murmured, looking away thoughtfully, 'how many of you sound like school teachers. I used to be like a little girl, too, I'd do everything I was told by bastards like you. But I'd be dead or in the Cabana if I had followed instructions. Instead, I made my own deal. Now I am exercising one of the options with you.'

'What do you mean, you'd be dead if you had followed our instructions?'

'Do you know what's in that file?'

'No.'

'I do. I wasn't supposed to, but I do. That's where you go wrong, because you have to depend on amateurs like me and we do what we feel like. Only an idiot would steal something and not even look to see what it was, and besides, Washington is a long way away.'

'Get back to the point.'

'There would have been such a stink when those papers were discovered missing that even Fidel would not be safe. They will tear that city and everyone in it apart. Now, why should I stay here and get killed, can you tell me? And why wasn't I allowed to microfilm the papers? Wouldn't that be the usual procedure? You know it would.'

'I can only guess, but probably someone wanted the

88

original paper for chemical tests in order to verify its authenticity.'

'You've read the personnel file on me, I'm sure, so you know that I grew up in the States, you know that I've had lovers, that I've received some money ... a lot of things that would lead any counter-intelligence officer to suspect me if the motivation was escalated high enough. Now if you were me, and you were asked to steal something that would shake a whole country, would you stay on afterwards?'

Guerin said he would, if those were his orders, and Julia made it apparent she either disbelieved him or thought him a fool. In truth, he was beginning to sweat, and not entirely because the storm was loading the air in the closed-off room with moisture which ran down the walls as though it were a cave. The girl was right, she should not have been asked to stay ... unless she was being handed over. She looked at him disconcertingly, as though she knew what was going through his mind.

'When I figured that much out,' Julia went on, 'I naturally wondered what was to keep you from killing me here, on the beach so to speak, and taking the papers with you.'

'You have us confused with the other side, don't you?'

'Oh, come on, you're all bastards and you know it. You mean to tell me you don't murder when you have to?'

Guerin smiled in spite of himself. He lit up a damp cigar, and was a little surprised to find his hands shaking. 'That's not my area of expertise, no, but of course it has been done under special circumstances.' He explained, 'It's relative between us and them.'

'Goddamned relative.'

He glanced at his watch again and stood up. 'That's it, you've had all the time I have to give.'

'You aren't even curious where the file is?'

'Whoever recruited you, for God's sake?'

'I don't have it anymore. I gave it to someone.'

89

'Then you're as good as dead.'

'No, I don't think so. If you take me out with you, I have a way of getting it back.'

'In other words, the price is going up?'

'You would think that,' she told him, without looking at him and with surprising bitterness. 'My price is exactly what it was—a way out of this crazy island and whatever salary you owe me.'

Guerin found it hard to know what to think, or to believe that the girl was simply a stringer, an ordinary scuffler out on the fringe of the game. For one thing, her obdurate bargaining in the face of a time factor which had now become crucial. He had done that to recalcitrants himself in the past, played the clock game, forcing them to sit and sweat when their lives depended upon movement, gambling and bluffing recklessly, and always winning—until now. 'Why have you done all this?'

'I told you, I thought they might send an assassin. But if I can get back into the States, then I don't think you'll hurt me. It would be easy here, but messy there.'

'You must have some reason for believing this.'

She shrugged. 'That's the kind of a reputation your people have nowadays ... since they started killing each other.' She noted the change in Guerin's expression and found it encouraging; he was frightened. 'That sort of madness seeps down to even the lowest level. I'm the lowest level.'

'I'll take you out,' Guerin decided. 'My orders were not to without the papers. I must know when you'll have them to give over.'

'In Miami, no later than the day after tomorrow. If you took people's word, I would give it.'

She had a small suitcase; Guerin grasped it and started for the door. Julia stopped him when his hand was on the latch, moving around in front of him to give the knocking signal he had heard used earlier.

'You have to do that even to get out?'

'It's okay, Paco,' she called softly through the door before opening it. Turning to Guerin: 'It's for your protection mostly.'

When they emerged, the peasant boy moved away from the shuttered window to meet them, grinning. From one hand dangled a huge .45 calibre Colt automatic, US Army issue, almost too much to lift. In passing, she told Guerin she had asked the boy to stay behind the window and kill him if he threatened her. 'He was more than willing to do that, too,' she added happily.

Looking at the boy now it was easy to see that he was not altogether bright. Guerin cursed quietly but sincerely —that would have been a particularly stupid way to die.

'Go get the old man,' Julia ordered the boy, and he started towards the road, which was almost visible through the unhealthy vegetation which separated it from the hut.

Paco never reached the line of trees, and instead was nearly bowled over by the lawyer, who came running towards them, whitefaced with eyes bulging, crying out in a strangled whisper: '*Milicianos!* Coming on the road.' Behind him was the old man, expressionless but with legs churning disjointedly and a heartbeat Guerin could mark across a hundred yards. There was no question of waiting for them; Julia grabbed Guerin's hand and pulled him after her, and he went without hesitation. It was a part of his profession to set priorities of life and death.

9

With every reason to assume they were running for their lives, Guerin and the girl travelled a torturous mile inland and eastward, some of it through swamp, before they went to ground in a stand of pines which Julia said had been planted by young communist pioneers to prevent soil erosion.

'How do you know that?' he asked her absently, while thinking about how they would never make the pickup point now and would have to wait until the next night.

'I've been stuck out here for two weeks. I wasn't going to sit around and listen to that son-of-a-bitch of a lawyer all day so I wandered up and down the coast, deciding where I would go if there was trouble.'

Guerin left off planning and analysing long enough to tell her that any underground organization which allowed people it was hiding to go wandering around the countryside deserved to be exterminated.

'And yet here you are,' she reminded him, 'and I'm the one who brought you.'

Despite an ankle swollen from an encounter with something anonymous and hard in the swamp, in spite of the fact that it was beginning to rain and they were being hunted as enemies of a state efficient in hunting and in which they were temporarily imprisoned, Guerin smiled.

The moist fetid soil he lay upon crept through his clothes and then his body and made him as miserable physically as he had ever been in his life. It would be that way for a long time and there was nothing to do but settle into it, absorb it, ignore it. He studied the girl he had come a thousand miles to save, for reasons he had not been allowed to understand. She was scarcely breathing hard after their run, and the smooth, rare-boned face showed nothing but a few scratches from the swamp. Guerin was an urban creature and not particularly physical, but then, according to what he had seen in her dossier, that was Julia, too, indeed more so. He remembered the marvellous way she moved when they were escaping; running, she was as fleet and graceful as one of the long-legged timid animals.

They waited through an eternity in silence, listening for the sounds of pursuit—presumably no one else would be out at this hour in the country in the rain—or for any sign of what happened to the other people who had been at the hut with them. They heard nothing, no shouting, no gunfire, and because it was out of the question that they return there, Guerin never found out what had happened. In retrospect, he thought it was probable that either the old man had mistaken a truckload of *campesinos* coming from some function and precipitated a panic, or perhaps they were *milicianos*, but bent on some business that had nothing to do with what was going on at the hut. One thing that seemed predictable was that the boy, Paco, was light-headed enough to use his toy-real pistol had it been a raid. Personally, Guerin felt nothing either way—he could not afford to—they had been the worse kind of amateurs, unredeemed either by passion or intelligence. He had seen such people die before, it was enough to be spared that.

He had once attended a two-week jungle survival course given by the Special Forces in Panama, and come away with little more than the conviction that he would much rather die than eat raw snakemeat again, but now for the first time was able to put some of the things they had learned to use. By breaking off young trees and pounding branches into the ground a framework was built. Across the top was stretched his waterproof jacket as a support

93

for a pine bough roof. Fortunately he had dragged Julia's small suitcase the entire way, not because he had thought the contents worth the struggle but simply to prevent its becoming a marker for pursuers, and it provided clothes to be used as something to keep out the rain and matting for the ground. He even managed to squeeze into her extra sweater, feeling foolish but grateful. 'You look very nice in magenta,' she told him sweetly, and he was still grateful. There was also a bar of Swiss chocolate to be shared, especially welcome in that they would probably not eat until they had rendez-voused with the boat the next night.

Guerin was sanguine when he explained to Julia that the boat was coming back at a predetermined time and there was every reason to believe that he would still be able to get her off the island. In his own mind he could imagine a lot of reasons why that might not happen, but it would have been stupid to let her know; he did not want to be abandoned, betrayed or to die in his sleep. And it was easier to lie than to stay awake twenty-four more hours. Her large green eyes, easily seen even in that claustrophobic darkness, looked straight at him as he explained, but they gave nothing away. She said she believed him. In the end, they curled up together out of necessity and fell into an exhausted slumber.

Guerin awoke first, stiff, bone-tired and hungry. It was impossible to move without waking the girl, but the weight of her body was almost pleasant enough to cancel out the other discomforts and he decided that the freedom to move around would not be better than this. Who or what she was did not particularly interest him any longer, would not be an issue again until they were off the island.

The wind had blown aside most of their cover. Lying on his back he could see that the clouds were breaking up and the wind had diminished; the rain seemed to have stopped somewhat earlier without greatly soaking the ground. With the first rays of the sun a mist rose up from the floor of pine needles on which they had lain. Guerin, frozen where he was, idled a hand through them to pick up a fistful of soil and let it drain back through his fingers. It was black and rich like most of the soil of Cuba, and if history were just or even logical the people of this place ought to be among the richest and most satisfied. He tried to work it around in his mind so that he could imagine the side of the game he represented bringing that correction about. It did not bend that way, but of course economic considerations were only a dangerous step removed from political concerns, and that was the sort of luxurious thinking he could not allow himself if he were to keep his professional objectivity. When they assigned you to a political action desk, that was the time, when your function justified it, to consider both sides of every question.

The girl stirred finally and that gave him something else to think about. 'Thank God,' he greeted her, 'my arm's been asleep so long gangrene's setting in.' She smiled appreciatively.

They spent the whole day in the place where they had slept, cooked by the damp heat which had followed the storm front in and without any real food at all. Guerin could, at least with the threat of danger as a stimulus, do nothing for long periods of time, but it almost drove the girl crazy. By early afternoon he was forced to talk to her continuously to keep her mind off her troubles. She was not one to suffer quietly and it seemed preferable to discuss mutually rather than listen to her complain individually.

'I am strictly a social person,' she pouted, 'I like lots of people, men especially, and music and laughter and noise. You're different, anyone could see that you are a lonely man who hates people.'

Guerin grinned self-consciously. 'Is it that apparent?'

'To me, it is. It gives me the creeps, actually, to see how you can lie there for two hours without hardly moving a muscle. And you're not even hungry, and, my God, my stomach thinks my throat has been cut from one ear to the other.'

'You were poor when you were a kid, you must have experienced hunger.'

'Why do you think I can't stand it now? You, I suppose you were rich?'

'Moderately,' Guerin agreed.

Julia shook her head. 'And yet you don't feel anything. I could hate you for that.'

'I have to have some professional skills.'

'Your profession ...' she said, as though it were an obscenity.

'It happens to be yours too, at the moment.'

'Not me, I was recruited. Then, when I'd done some things that could send me right to the firing wall, your nice friends refused to let me quit.'

'We have to do that sometimes. Everybody does.'

She raised her voice a little and he signalled for her to lower it, but she went on giving off the same heat at fewer decibels. 'Why the hell are you always talking about other guys, the communists, I suppose you mean, although somehow you don't seem to have the guts to say it ... anyway, I haven't been caught by them ... yet. So all I know is what lousy bastards you are ...'

She trailed off and sulked for a while. Guerin had been watching some cane workers in the distance He turned back to the girl to ask conversationally, 'Julia, why did you join us?' It was the first time he had used her name, he realized.

'I never joined you. I just did what I did.'

'You're an American citizen.'

'No one consulted me about it. Anyway, I am also a Cuban citizen.'

'Why don't you just tell me the truth, why you allowed yourself to be recruited.'

'Because it's none of your goddamned business, but I will tell you anyway. There was a boy—yes, I call him that, he was younger than me—but he had fought in the revolution, in the city underground where they were all middle class kids. Actually his family was quite rich, and it was the only kind of spirit we had here in the years after the revolution that made it possible for us to even know each other, much less love each other. I loved him,' she specified. 'His family hated the idea of course, but, you know, they were scared like all the *gusanos* so they kept their mouths shut. He was beautiful, though. I've had a lot of men, but nobody I loved before, or anyone so beautiful as that boy. Victorio.'

That seemed to be all she wanted to say about it, but after a decent interval Guerin asked, 'What happened to him?'

'They killed him.'

'Who?'

'The *Fidelistas*. The revolutionaries. The thing he had fought for ate him, like a lot of others.'

'Was he innocent?'

'What does that matter? No, he was not—they had to kill him, I guess, from their point of view. But that's when I joined you.'

'What will you do back home?'

She shrugged non-committally.

'Hey,' he warned, 'stay behind that tree, will you. The light's changing and they may be able to see you.'

'I don't care right now.'

They lapsed back into silence for a while, with the girl staring openly at Guerin. He was aware of it and it made him slightly uncomfortable, but then she was as direct as any girl he had ever known. 'And don't move around so much,' he told her out of the corner of his mouth. 'And keep your voice down.'

When a little mongrel nosed its way into the thicket,

barking, she tried to play with it, irritating Guerin more than he was free to admit. He kicked the dog to encourage it to leave, and Julia glared at him. Matter-of-factly, he told her that he would have had to strangle it if it had refused to go. 'If it's some kind of moral dilemma for you, I suggest it's rationally preferable the dog gets a kick in the ass to your receiving a bullet through the eye.'

'How much is your salary?' she asked him out of no-where.

Guerin laughed at the mercurial way she had of shifting ground, and she admitted it was not a bad laugh for a man like him.

'About twenty thousand a year and expenses.'

'That's a lot of money.'

'You haven't been home in a while. But why do you want to know?'

She shrugged, as if that were none of his business, or at least of no importance. When the cane workers went somewhere for a *siesta*—she said they looked like city people conscripted for agricultural work—he allowed her to move around and stretch her muscles. 'I just wondered,' she answered, getting around to it finally, 'how much it cost them to get a man like you to do these things. I know enough to know that you must be a good agent—especially if they send you on this—so you must have been at it for a long time.'

'Eight years. That's long for us.'

'It's your career, then.'

'It's what I do best. How I think of myself. It's also a steady income, an expense account, an insurance policy, retirement fund, friends, a big organization whose successes or failures you identify with, a set of ethics—admittedly highly special—gossip, a lot of gossip, probably too much, and even pretty girls at the water cooler. Also, an annual Christmas party, if you happen to be "in house".'

'You're making fun of me,' she said agreeably, 'but I

don't mind—it proves at least that you are human. Do you suppose it's the same for the ones on the "other side", as you call it?'

'Sure. For the KGB and GRU anyway. I don't know about the people here ...'

'They are human too, you know,' she shot at him.

Guerin gave her a bemused look but otherwise his voice remained mild. 'I was just going to say that they probably run a little more on political fervour, but they'll professionalize as the regime settles in.' He sprayed around the insect repellent he had brought in the medical kit. It was a tiny container and he had wanted to reserve it for after dark when the waiting would be painful enough without hordes of mosquitos, but the dampness and the proximity of the swamp was making things uncomfortable even now. 'The Chinese, for a lot of reasons, the racial identification problem being the most obvious, but also I suppose having to do with doctrine, are largely amateur, defiantly amateur from what I hear.'

'Now you're giving me a lecture,' she complained, turning away in a calculated gesture.

Guerin felt oddly hurt by her reproof. In the beginning he would have preferred to have exercised his time in the usual manner, running conjugations or memory tests of various kinds through his head, solving complicated mathematical problems without writing them, evoking and re-enforcing bits of poetry or favourite quotations, but in the hours since they had begun to talk he had grown to like it somehow, liked even her hostility.

'Goddamn, watch it!' he hissed suddenly. An old man, a real peasant, had come towards the trees from the cane field and was almost upon them without their seeing him. Guerin spent ten seconds looking around for an alternative and then threw himself over the girl to hold her down, masking her mouth with his hand. With all his will he tried to grind the two of them down into the ground out

99

of sight. The old man came on. Julia's eyes were open, two great green moons of terror and anger that shifted from the old man, looming gigantically on top of them, to Guerin, whose responsibility it was to save them.

Guerin himself had sorted out his options. Once it was too late to run for it, it was too late to make an open fight for it. So the gun in his jacket pocket remained there, out of sight and mind. If the old man settled in for a *siesta*, they could simply try to wait him out. Or it might be worth the risk to garrotte him, on the assumption that at his age and state of general enfeeblement he might not be missed until later, and they would still have a chance to make the rendez-vous. Of course, if they were caught that would mean certain execution. Guerin chose the former; unfortunately, he admitted to himself, out of weakness, because he had no stomach for the act.

The old man stopped at the periphery of the grove of pines and settled down against a single laurel tree to drink something out of a jar. Guerin, if he raised himself a mere few inches, could see the back of that salt of the earth white head, which for him had the symbolic attributes of a snarling police dog, holding him in a cataleptic agony of suspense. Gradually, as much to free himself from mental paralysis, he rolled off the girl and removed his hand from her mouth. It was not necessary to do anything more to convey the imperativeness of strict silence; her pale face and narrow breathing reassured him. She had looked much braver when they had run for their lives from the *milicianos*, but then, to be honest, so had he; a running man was still a free man, whatever the danger.

When he lowered the side of his head back into its depression in the pine needles they lay face to face, inches removed from each other, so that he could feel her breath as the only compensation he would have for the rest of that memorably terrible day. Insects made cracking noises in the heat around them while occasionally one buzzed into their eyes and ears, and the sweat ran down to form a damp padding under their cheeks. He was surprised, although he should not have been, to find that she was wearing eye makeup, for it ran in pitiable rivulets down her face, grotesque and yet somehow appealing, like a failed harlequin. That seemed so Cuban, to put on makeup while hiding from the police through swamps and fields and near-jungles. He would have smiled if he had been less frightened. With the slight movement of the forearm which she had placed under her head, the way a child might sleep, her hand reached out far enough to touch his, and Guerin was affected beyond anything he would have believed possible.

Once, after a half hour, or an hour or two hours, he again raised his head and saw a *miliciano* crossing the space between them and the cane field with a Russian submachine gun suspended loosely from his shoulder by a strap. The *miliciano* waved at the old man and the old man waved back. The option based on weakness had probably been the right one—the others would have missed him. The old man stayed a long time after that, in no hurry to get back to the travail of the harvest, however glorious and romantic Havana radio might picture it. But then at last he stood up. To urinate, as it turned out. To Guerin's mind, it took fully fifteen minutes for him to rebutton his pants. Once that was over he sighed contentedly—they could hear it, he was that close—and marched his ancient bones back into the fight.

When they felt free to breathe, to move, to start life again, it was almost too painful. A good five minutes was spent pulling the badly atrophied human machine to the functioning vertical position it had once spent millions of years to reach, and even then they bent slightly like the apes. At the sight of each other, hunched and dangling, they laughed, and that too was excruciating. At sunset, before dark, before they could even be sure the cane workers had gone, they gave themselves over to the reaction that came from what they had suffered, and ran, recklessly, staggering, shivering, down to the south coast.

It was Guerin's estimate that they had fled from the hut in a direction that was as much easterly as it was north, or inland. In returning to the beach it was possible to skirt the marsh, highly desirable considering the state of his swollen ankle, which was already showing some signs of infection. He was going now on the pain-killers he had brought in the medical kit. Julia, from the moment when she was free of the hiding place, became exhilarated, almost manic, and ran like a child. She would rush ahead, then have to return to him as he limped and lurched along. She was undisguisedly solicitous and he felt himself, against all his instincts, touched by it. In the end, for the last few hundred yards to the beach, she actually helped to support him.

They reached the pickup point an hour after dark without, as far as they knew, having crossed paths with anyone. There were five hours more to be waited amidst the blowing grass of the dunes and under a neon moon which would make it impossible to escape should a patrol come upon them, particularly with Guerin hobbled as he was.

Played out, no longer caring, they lay on their backs and stared silently at the cosmic timepiece of the planets and stars. Occasionally Julia asked him a question about one of them or a configuration of them, and he expressed surprise and a certain delight to find that she knew anything at all concerning what he considered his personal esoterica. A little of the sheen came off it when he found out it was because her Cuban grandmother had been an astrologist.

Since he could no longer do very much about evasion, Guerin's principal worry was that he had chosen the wrong place to wait—it was the same little spit of land where he had come across the old man with the flashlight.

Blue had hit it wrong previously but it seemed reasonable that he would not repeat his mistake in diamond-bright weather. Guerin's decision had to take into consideration the personality of the Cuban pilot; was he rigid, could he admit the mistake of the night before even to himself? If not, and he returned obdurately to the point where he had deposited his agent previously, then they would probably miss it and be on their way to the Cabana within a fortnight. Ultimately it was the fact that Sandy was aboard that decided him.

Around eleven, Julia started and gripped his arm. He asked her what it was with a studied casualness.

'I thought I heard guns firing. Out there.' She pointed towards the ocean.

Guerin made the effort of pushing himself to one elbow and cranking up an ear. There was a cut in the dunes directly in front of them which provided a view down to the water, but he saw nothing out there to challenge its awesome opaqueness except for the breaking waves. 'I didn't hear it,' he said. 'It's a pretty good surf tonight—it could have been that.'

'No, it was guns. You get to know what they sound like in Cuba.'

She was right, Guerin had heard it too. And it was ominous, because this close to pickup time their boat had to be out there somewhere. 'The wind is offshore,' he told her, 'and a fire-fight close enough in to be heard could also be seen.'

She did not look convinced. He settled back. There was nothing to do but to lay there and smell the warm things the wind had brought, mimosa and gardenia and hibiscus mixed with the rich melted earth of Cuba, the smell of the sun at midnight. Nothing else to do but wait.

The clear night saved them. Blue used his head and brought the boat in midway between his previous landing point and the place where he should have been, and the distances were such that with a little effort he was visible from both. Guerin had managed to keep his nerves in rein until now but the sight of the boat nearly drove him wild with joy; grabbing Julia by one wrist he dragged her, running and stumbling, out of the dunes and down the beach. The suffering ankle was forgotten and when the sand sucked off one of his shoes he left it.

The boat's bow nuzzled into the beach with the surf breaking over the stern, but it looked as imperturbable as a resting pelican. Blue was standing up straight at the conning position, searching the beach in both directions for signs of trouble, his hands down and out of sight, but no doubt on the throttle and the wheel. Homer crouched on the bow, next to the 20-mm, his machine pistol cradled lazily under one arm, watching them come. For one terrifying moment Guerin wondered if this was it, if the gunner would simply cut them in two as they waded out. If that was the man's assignment, he would never have a better chance. Guerin slowed them to a measured approach and put one hand into his jacket pocket, although he could not imagine what good that would do unless he was allowed to take his assassin with him, and he was not the sort to take much consolation from that. Homer surprised him by waving for them to hurry up.

They were almost into the surf before Guerin saw it—a line of bullet holes marched neatly across the bulkhead just aft of the cabin. His computer instantly and efficiently ticked off the relevant observations and filed them without comment: automatic weapon ... small calibre ... probably a hand gun ... Further back, close to the stern, some more holes, probably from a pistol or a carbine. The crew of a Cuban patrol boat might be carrying any kind of weaponry imaginable, but somehow it had missed at close range with its deck guns, apparently. His conscious mind was struggling with something more important, something missed. 'Where is Fox?' he shouted above the inrushing water, while boosting the girl up into Homer's large capable hands.

'We had trouble, hurry up!' He turned away to take Julia back along the narrow deck to the stern. Guerin scrambled up on his own, whacking the swollen ankle cruelly on the steel sides of the boat but scarcely feeling it in his anxiety to find out what had happened to his friend.

He leaped down on to the afterdeck and spun Homer around. 'What the hell happened to Fox?' he shouted again, this time straight into the man's face. Homer took the time, and the prerogative, to signal Blue to take the boat out. Then he turned slowly and looked down at Guerin, the muzzle of his machine pistol bumping gently against the latter's chest simply by virtue of his proximity. Julia looked on, not understanding the content but with wise eyes for trouble. Guerin felt, for an instant, embarrassed, reduced by the trivia of the situation, his swollen ankle and one bare foot, the soaked clothes, wild hair and unshaven face ... self-conscious, foolish, impotent—he knew what had happened to Sandy.

'He's dead. I put him over the side,' Homer said.

10

By Homer's account, the action had begun well out beyond territorial limits when the Cubans, in an admittedly older, slower boat, had come up on them from behind. They were able to get into range without being seen because of their low silhouette and the general choppiness of the water.

'What the hell kind of excuse is that?' Guerin demanded

with considerable heat. 'When a trained agent with years of experience is killed, you don't just say we didn't happen to be looking that way. There'll be an inquiry, I'm telling you that right now. I'm requesting one.' He slammed his fist into his hand in an uncharacteristic gesture of frustration.

Homer allowed just the suggestion of a smile to play close to his lips. 'It was Fox back here. I was on the bow shaking down the 20-mm for the run in. It was his responsibility.'

'We'll never hear that from him, will we?' Guerin said, angry with himself for its lameness. He wanted literally to strike out and kill the weapons man, and the aimless intensity of that feeling made everything he said, or might say, sound fatuous to him.

'Nope, I guess not,' agreed Homer, glancing aside casually to where Julia sat huddled a few feet away by the stern, puffing on a cigarette. Guerin followed his eyes and felt a pang of sympathy for the intense weariness which creased the girl's face. Still, he resented the distraction and Homer's indifference to his questions more than he cared how Julia felt. 'He was careless and now he's dead,' Homer summed up, swinging back to confront Guerin.

'As the bodyguard, you don't feel any responsibility?'

'Why should I? You know what he did when they opened up? Stood straight up and fired back with that little Schmeisser. What that got him, it took me fifteen minutes and three buckets of water to clean up.'

There was no reason to believe that Julia either could, or cared to hear what they were saying, but Guerin thought he caught her in an almost imperceptible shiver out of the corner of his eye.

'You say he was an experienced agent,' Homer went on, 'but he wasn't much good for combat.'

'No,' Guerin said, 'he had never been in combat.'

'But you have,' Homer posed, looking at him as if to measure him for a suit.

'Yes.' Then, as if he felt impelled to erect a moral qualifier between himself and the other man, he added: 'I didn't like it.'

Homer shrugged. 'Anyway,' he went on, 'Blue kept his head and brought the bow around so I could get a whack at them with the twenty. They folded and ran.'

'Why wasn't there an alarm? We're not out of it yet, and this area should be crawling with ships and planes.'

Homer said he did not know: either the boat did not have a radio, it had been no more than a large speedboat really, or the tack they had assumed directly after the engagement, heading away from the island, had fooled the Hostiles into thinking they had had enough. Besides, you could never expect Cubans to behave rationally under combat conditions.

'You took a hell of a chance coming in after that.'

The weapons man flashed a grin and Guerin almost liked it for its surprising expansiveness, even if the words that accompanied it were a banal mockery: 'In the best traditions of the Service we saw our duty and we did it. Couldn't leave you to the *parodonistos*, Mercator.'

Guerin thanked him perfunctorily and went over to try and talk Julia into sleeping. She refused, saying she would sleep when they reached land, any land, and asked him to stay and discuss whatever was interesting to him, so long as it was trivial and had nothing to do with their present circumstances. Homer moved around attending to his duties, but Guerin felt his eyes on them continuously.

Eventually, at dawn, when they were well out of the danger zone, Homer packed away his weapons and went to sleep on a mat on the floor. Whether or not he was really sleeping was of small concern to Guerin as he climbed up to the conning position to see the little Cuban captain who had brought him out. The man's eyes were blood-red from the continuous strain and his face wore a stubbled, sun-scarred mask. He did not even look aside when Guerin came next to him.

'I want to thank you,' Guerin said to him in Spanish. 'Especially for coming back.'

'That was what I was paid for.'

'Nevertheless, you had an excuse, you didn't have to.'

The Cuban said nothing and Guerin clapped him on the shoulder in what, for him, was a rare familiar gesture. 'You are a good sailor and a brave man.'

'Thank you.'

'During the fire-fight, were you frightened?'

'Frightened? Of course.'

'You've been in them before?'

'More than once,' he said without feeling, but then his voice changed slightly. 'I am sorry ... about your friend.'

'Homer says he fought well. That he got off several clips and maybe killed a couple of the bastards. That it is thanks to Fox that we are all alive.'

The Cuban nodded confirmation. Guerin studied him for a moment, then went back down to the deck to think that over.

When they pulled into the lagoon at Manna Key, the entire personnel turned out to meet them, presumably because incoming missions were considered less of a security risk than outgoing. Homer had taken over for Fox at the radio and sent a code signal ahead which announced the success of the mission and their imminent return. Guerin allowed him to go ahead with it simply because he had no intention of discussing Julia's gambit at any but the highest levels.

He went up to say goodbye to Blue. 'Where will you go now, old man?'

'To the Yucatan, I think. We run some people from there.'

'You make too many runs and fortune will turn you over to them.'

'She is hard on sailors, anyway. Besides, where can I earn this kind of money fishing?'

They shook hands and Blue looked him more or less in the eye to say, 'I am sorry.' Guerin thought he knew why now.

He went down to assist Julia into the dinghy. She had slept a bit in spite of her pledge but her face was even more constrained than before, and the lips, Guerin noted, were pale and tremulous. 'Relax,' he told her, 'you're not facing execution anymore.'

'What makes you so sure?'

Guerin realized that she meant it. 'Look, I don't know exactly what you've done to us, but I wish you'd cut all this crap out about the kind of people we are.'

'Why don't you grow up?' she snapped, and he was amused to hear how, a few feet from American soil, the years in Cuba had dropped totally out of her speech.

Homer pushed them off and said goodbye to Julia. She returned it politely. For his group leader he had a wave and a big grin. 'Goodbye, you murdering bastard,' Guerin murmured to himself, but otherwise he stared back without responding, his face tightly wound, as grey and cold as death. Homer's smile faded, and they looked across the water at each other honestly, for what they were. Julia glanced back at Homer, and then at Guerin, impressed by the intensity of the feeling underlying the hard promises they were making to each other.

'Why do you hate him?' she asked.

Guerin's voice was thick: 'That's none of your business. A moment later he softened it. 'There's that trouble among us; I mean, in our organization. You're better off not knowing about it.'

'I do know about it. I told you.'

'Then forget about what you know.'

She shook her head.

'Jesus, you beg for trouble everywhere, don't you?'

'No. I'm just a victim,' she told him, then added: 'Like you.'

Guerin's voice was querulous. 'Like me?'

Julia did not look as though she would explain anyway, but at that moment they reached the dock and were assisted ashore by a couple of men who may or may not have been sailors, but were wearing whites and dealt with the boat with ease and familiarity. Burke stepped forward and shook Guerin's hand. Indicating Julia, he asked, 'This the one, huh?' Guerin acknowledged that it was, and noted the Commandant surveying them closely for some sort of sign of what they were supposed to bring out with them. 'Guess you had a rough time from the looks of the boat. You get what you wanted?'

'Fox is dead,' Guerin answered. 'I want transport for DC right away.'

'Sure. Sorry.'

They all walked up to the main bungalow, Julia keeping her eyes to the ground and the personnel watching her, even in her filthy, ragged slacks and sweater, like a flock of fascinated penguins. Burke said that actually he had radioed for the plane to take them out the moment he received Homer's signal announcing that they were clear and incoming. 'I've had three inquiries about the mission from different people back at the plant since you left here. Pretty damned unusual.' Guerin simply grunted his agreement that it was unusual. The other news he took more seriously, that he was ordered to proceed first to Miami and report to the resident there first hand.

He argued it out on the porch for fifteen minutes with Burke. 'Something's come up ... something nobody knows about but me. I insist on going straight through to DC.'

'Insist till hell freezes over, the plane that comes in here has orders to go only as far as Miami. You report anything wrong to the resident and he can have it on the tube home in a few minutes, if he has to. But that's where you'll go to start with.'

'I won't get on the goddamned plane,' Guerin told him quietly. He could see that Burke was growing red, and in part because the rest of the people on the station were watching them argue. He wished they would go inside if they were going to carry on with it, but the Commandant had planted himself firmly in front of the entrance to the bungalow, determined to see it through on that spot.

'Then I'll tell you the same thing you told that nigger out there before you went, you go under orders or I have you removed from the station in chains. Go easy or hard, it's up to you.'

'Under whose authority?'

'I have my orders. They're very explicit.'

'From who? Whose orders specifically, dammit?'

'From the head of my department,' he almost shouted. 'You know I can't give you a name.'

'Oh, my God . . .' Guerin came close to laughing. He decided suddenly to give in. Burke had been around a long time; he knew there was something wrong with that kind of victory.

They were given fresh clothes and an opportunity to shower. Burke did not come to dinner, which was served only to Julia and Guerin on the terrace of the main building by the Cuban houseboy. She wore outsized men's clothes but the glory of her rich dark skin against the whites brought Guerin a long way out of the depression he felt at the way things were going. It was only when they sat down that he realized she had not spoken since they had set foot on American soil.

'I have nothing in particular to celebrate,' she explained when he queried her.

'You're alive.'

'That's the least anyone can be. Happiness ought to start somewhere better than that.'

'Very nice,' he said, smiling. 'On top of everything else you say things like that.'

She frowned. 'There are times, in the company of men like you, when I hope the communists win, because what they say about you is true.'

Guerin inexplicably found himself blushing. 'I'm sorry, I didn't mean it to sound that way. I just happen to know a lot about your background, which I grant isn't normal, I mean between a man and a woman, but it's my job and built into the situation, so it can't be helped, can it? If I find you full of contradictions, if you're a lot brighter and more complicated than you have any right to be considering that background, well why in hell should you get mad about it. It's a compliment, for Christ's sake isn't it? What's more interesting in people than those kind of surprises, for God's sake ... Goddammit, I'm getting mad just explaining it to you.' He broke off with a self-conscious laugh, and to his surprise she joined in.

'You know, you blushed.'

'It's not the first time.'

'Well, I think it's a first time for me. It can't be very common among spies.'

He concentrated on his food. 'You're getting silly now.'

'The other one, the black, is he gone?'

Guerin indicated the lagoon—it was empty. 'They must have left while we were cleaning up.'

'Don't you know when or where they went?'

'It's not my business to know. They're no longer under my command.'

'Only me.'

Guerin nodded soberly. He knew she was not being cute and feminine in saying it. 'What is it about him?' he asked.

'On the boat, when you were talking to the captain, he

tried to find out if I had the file.'

'He shouldn't have known anything about it.'

'That's what I thought. Your friend, the one who was killed, they threw his body overboard?'

'Yes.'

'Did he have a family?'

'A wife and two children. I know them,' he added.

'And yet you didn't seem to care about that. You were mad at Homer about a lot of things I don't understand, but not about that.'

'No, you see ... it's hard to explain, but that kind of solution is customary.' He paused, a little discomfited by his own choice of words. 'This way, he died in a storm at sea while fishing or whatever the cover story is, and his wife gets the pension from an anonymous trust fund. But you take an agent's body back to his home town and a lot of people let their emotions run away with them. They want to know everything, they get self-righteous about it even when they knew what the dead man was doing for a living in the first place, so then they start talking to reporters and the like and pretty soon a lot of absurd speculation appears in feature stories in newspapers or magazines. And, of course, the Firm can't answer it no matter how detrimental it is.'

'That's still very stupid. And heartless.'

'Dead is dead. I'll put in for a service medal for him.'

'I hope it does you all a lot of good.'

Guerin looked guilty. 'Even less than you imagine. It's entirely symbolic, on paper. His wife will never be allowed to hold it after it's conferred, because our medals are just not for showing—to anyone.'

'You must do me a favour.' Her large eyes were on him, her voice confidential, and for a ridiculous moment Guerin's heart beat rapidly at the thought of doing anything at all that might please her. 'If, after I've delivered this tremendously important file to you, your superiors think I am a big American heroine, don't let them reward me with that medal. If they do, I'll be pleased to spit on it and hand it back with the suggestion they flush it down the White House toilet.'

When Guerin poured another glass of beer, he had to struggle to disguise the trembling of his hand. The source of his terror—and it was that—was the realization that momentarily he had shared her attitudes.

Captain Cespedes was on a tour of inspection of jails and prisons in Oriente Province when a report came to him suggesting that a clerk in the Department of the Interior named Julia Fernandez had left the island by illegal means. Several incidents were listed on the report which were thought might correlate with her disappearance, including the diversionary signal fire and a gun battle which ended fatally for a half-wit boy wielding a US Army issue forty-five and thought to be a tool of counter-revolutionary forces.

Cespedes had known the approximate area in which Julia was hiding, but none of the particulars of her escape. Nor had he wanted to; he had enough confidence in the Yankees to assume they would get her off. Now it remained for him to hurry back to Havana and try to find out from his 'apparat' in the Southeastern United States whether or not she had taken her secrets out with her.

11

The seaplane came in just as dinner ended. They watched in silence as it cut a silver furrow across the black mirror of the lagoon, before going inside to collect their things. At the last moment Burke tried to separate Guerin from his charge, insisting that new instructions had come in to the effect that Julia was to remain behind for a later plane. Guerin wanted it in writing, or at the very least a letter from Burke assuming full responsibility, which the latter insisted was an assault upon his honour and something for which there was no precedent. Both of those things, Guerin admitted, were true.

There was a great deal of acrimonious talk back and forth, but in the end she went with Guerin because he had no intention of losing sight of her until the documents were in his possession and was willing to take risks. Neither Burke nor any of his staff came down to the water's edge to watch them go, but Guerin had learned to live his life without anything resembling sentiment.

As the plane taxied out across the flat water it needed for take-off, Julia looked back at the still-life of Manna Key. 'Not much of a send-off, considering how glad they were to see us.'

'There are worse ways to leave a place like this.' She looked at him to see what he meant. 'We got our way. We were lucky,' he said.

With a frantic roar the little plane bounced off the surface, clawed at the black air, slammed back into the water in a movement so jarring it caused Julia to cry out and both men to grunt with pain and shock, but then finally, with the encircling reef looming critically close, it seemed to flap its way up again and soared out across the Caribbean.

'Routine,' the pilot said, grinning. He crammed a stick of gum into his mouth and offered some to his passengers. Manna, perennially under dimout conditions, had already disappeared into the night sea.

Julia withdrew into her peajacket and seemed to sleep, but Guerin remained alert. He watched the pilot's instruments over his shoulder for the answer as to where they were going. He was not anxious to repeat the itinerary of his trip down; there was a possible hazard in stopping off at various stations where conflicting elements might be in control. But within minutes the red glow from the panel revealed a course east by north-east—they were headed out around the Atlantic tip of Cuba, the windward passage over Haiti, and that could only mean a direct flight to Miami. Guerin asked the pilot if that were the case but the man refused to confirm it—not that it mattered. Pilots, the agent knew, were invariably sports oriented, and that's how the residue of the night was spent, discussing pro football and baseball in a tiny airplane running without lights, radio contact, or registered flight plan at eleven thousand feet around the eastern tip of Cuba. He could only hope this boyishly unconcerned flyer knew the warp and woof of the Continental Defence Command.

This time he was taken directly into Miami Bay and to the landing ramp of a boat and seaplane service company, SEFAS (South Eastern Florida Air and Sea), which served as principal cover for the functional operations of the Firm in that area. They were met by lower echelon personnel, who were courteous and offered them some early breakfast, which they refused by reason of their late dinner and extreme fatigue. The duty officer told them the resident would see them downtown at eleven and they were free to sleep upstairs in the company offices until that time. Guerin insisted Julia remain in the same room with him and she made no objection, nor did the staff seem to impart any sexual connotations to that, living, as they did, in a world where everybody watched everybody else all of the time. Once locked away, they fell asleep instantly in their clothes and were only awakened for their appointment with difficulty.

Julia still had her bag with her but she was given no time to change out of her navy issue clothes, and was restricted cosmetically to rinsing her face with cold water, which made her very grumpy on the way over. They were transported in an unmarked car driven by another Cuban. Guerin was quiet and thoughtful, and when Julia grumbled about the working conditions he told her to shut up. Anyway, a Cuban working for the Firm in Florida could very easily be a double and he did not want her identifying herself.

He was apprehensive about the meeting with Middlebrook; personally, he still believed the girl would come through on her promise; he had gone too far in trusting her already if she did not. Either way, he wanted the opportunity to follow up on it, if only to protect himself from the consequences. If she was lying he did not care who got hold of her, and he also knew the Firm would not be above handing her back.

They were dropped off in an alley behind the Cal-Way Corporation and escorted through the back hallways by a young man Guerin recognized as a code clerk on the Vienna station when he had been there. They exchanged greetings but that was all, for the young man was very brisk and businesslike; once they reached Middlebrook's outer office he was gone.

The resident came out to greet them like a small-town mayor. He pumped Julia's hand, calling her Estrellita, and told her how happy and relieved he felt now that she had been removed from that vulnerable position she had so courageously occupied in the Ministry of the Interior. Guerin wondered how much of the con or charm, or whatever Middlebrook thought it was, would survive the news that Julia did not have the file she had been ordered to steal. He sat them down and brought out the same bottle of bourbon. Julia did not hesitate to ask him if he had something more civilized, since they had not had lunch yet.

'Sorry, I'm an unreconstructed Southern boy, I guess. Bourbon's the only drink that seems moral to me, even though I haven't been home in twenty years.'

Guerin groaned inwardly, his nerves were gouging him and he did not see how he was going to be able to bear the personality cliches that obviously lay between them and confrontation with the crucial question.

Julia agreed to bourbon but otherwise she was not giving Middlebrook anything in the way of amenities. Considering what she had done and was about to announce, it was, Guerin thought, either a magnificent indifference to consequences or aggressiveness calculated to put her opponent off balance. The resident ran through a list of agents known to Julia, asking her opinion of their morale and effectiveness in turn, but her responses bordered on the monosyllabic. It was probable that Middlebrook was going through all this as countertactic; if the file was as important as it had been presented there was no rational reason why he would avoid asking for it the moment they walked into the room.

'We'll have to ask you to hang around for a little more de-briefing after we've settled this business,' the resident said to Julia. 'Maybe you'll remember things that escape you now.'

Guerin read it, it was a clumsy threat.

Middlebrook turned to him suddenly. 'I'm sorry about the man you lost, Mercator. I understand he was a friend of yours.'

'How did you know?' Guerin asked, though scarcely surprised.

'I get reports. Where are the papers you brought out?'

There was only the briefest agony of silence and then Guerin, anticipating Julia, plunged in. 'She didn't bring them with her. But she claims she'll be able to put her hands on them by tomorrow. Here, in Miami.'

The resident failed to blink, though tiny beads of sweat had been forming at the hairline for the last few minutes. Guerin was watching him closely, trying to determine whether or not the man had known beforehand. It was possible Homer had already guessed the truth when he had asked Julia about it on the way home. It was even possible that she had told him. Or word might have come out of Cuba somehow. There were a thousand ways, but Middlebrook was not giving away any of them. Julia remained in perfect control as the large man's eyes zeroed in on her.

'What is he telling me?'

'I should think it would be perfectly clear. I didn't bring the papers with me.'

'Did you even get them?' Middlebrook asked her sharply, giving himself away to Guerin, who now knew what the resident did not know.

'Of course,' Julia said. 'But I made other arrangements to get them out.'

'Knowing what we were going through to bring you out?'

'I thought you owed me that much.'

Her relentless cheek for some reason seemed to disconcert the resident, who would have had to have been exposed to a lot of it in his profession. He turned back to Guerin. 'You brought her out. Despite the fact that your orders said *with* the file, not without.'

'I played her as long as time allowed. Then there wasn't any other alternative but to take a chance she was telling me the truth.'

'You mean you lost your nerve.'

'When was the last time you were in Cuba?'

'That's insubordinate, Mercator.'

'Put it in your report.'

Julia was watching them with a bemused smile. Guerin should have been mad about it but he did not care at the moment.

The resident addressed Julia from between tightly drawn lips. 'What in hell made you think you could disobey orders and get away with it?'

She shrugged pleasantly and replied, 'I already have,' tossing back her long black hair in that quintessentially feminine gesture. Guerin thought, for the first time, that she might really be beautiful. Certainly she was brave, which was much the same thing.

'No, you haven't,' Middlebrook told her pointedly. He was one of those people who are only completed through anger.

'We only have to wait twenty-four hours, for Christ's sake,' Guerin put in. 'If she doesn't produce then you can do any goddamned extra-legal thing you want with her. Put her in the Bay, for all I care. Neither one of us is going to get canned between now and then.'

'Is that all you're worried about happening?' Middlebrook asked with deliberate archness, suggesting much more was possible. 'Why?' he demanded to know from Julia.

'I didn't trust you. No one does, any more.'

The resident threw up his hands, becoming momentarily an exasperated uncle. 'What the hell kind of answer is that? Who asked you to trust us? You took on a job, with responsibilities. And you didn't live up to them, now you're going to read us lectures about morality. I'm telling you something right now, sister—you may be a traitor, with your American citizenship. And you know what the penalty for that is?'

Julia looked monumentally unconcerned. Guerin was scornful. 'This girl is much too bright for that kind of crap. You're just wasting time.'

'She doesn't know people die in this trade?'

'She knows you're not going to take her in front of the Federal Grand Jury of Dade County, much less in DC. She knows you're not going to hurt her as long as she has the file; you have to think twice while she's inside the country, in any event, and you won't have any reason to after she gives it over.' He turned to look at Julia. 'I hope she knows that, that we're not simply gratuitous murderers.'

Julia smiled and said she knew no such thing.

It had become intensely hot in the room. Middlebrook stood with a great heaving sigh, as though air was escaping under pressure, and went to turn up the air conditioning. He raised the liquor bottle to his guests but they declined, so he poured himself another, using a glass lined with brown sediment from melted ice cubes. It was, Guerin recognized, a time for regrouping. Not particularly artful, none of it, but then the resident was a simple, angry man.

'Back to the matter of trust,' said Middlebrook suddenly. 'After working for us for years, doing a fair job, no big deals but getting paid regularly ...'

'Blackmail!' Julia snarled. 'After the first thing I did—Mother of God how I wish I hadn't—but after that it was all blackmail. And when I wanted to come out I was turned down flat. What did you care if I got killed?'

She was starting to get worked up, bored with the sang-froid she had adopted for whatever reason at the beginning of this. A real Latin, after all.

'I wasn't a regular agent, I didn't cost you fifty thousand dollars to train, just a nothing little chicana girl to you ... and a black one at that. You're probably *all* rednecks, you pack of bastards. So don't talk to me about duty and responsibilities and all that crap. I look out for Julia, because nobody else ever did.'

When she eased off, Middlebrook merely grumbled that he had not 'run' her personally, she had been entirely under Virgil in Key West and therefore he was not responsible for anything which had gone on in the past. He was lying, of course.

'I know Virgil,' Julia muttered to no one in particular. 'Shit on Virgil.'

Middlebrook drew himself up behind the desk and stared at her for a long moment. He made his decision right then.

'All right. You're free to make your contact as long as it's here in Miami. But I'm sending some people with you, wherever it is. You can go home, Mercator.'

Julia said, 'No!' She indicated Guerin. 'He's the only one I trust even a little bit. I don't want anyone else around when I pick it up.'

'I'm ordering you ...'

'Go to hell! He comes with me or I won't get them for you.'

Middlebrook turned away to look out the window, then spun back to give Guerin a hard look. 'You're in this with her!' he accused.

Guerin shook his head. 'I don't know what she's doing. But I share at least some of her suspicions, and I wouldn't go back to the plant without that file no matter what you ordered me to do.'

'You're shooting your whole career.'

'Maybe. But I can't be sure of that, any more than I can be sure of anything else currently. So I'll just do what I was sent to do. And hope.'

Middlebrook leaned forward like the chairman of the board. 'Your personal file's been optimum up to now, Mercator, unless someone's been selective in what they sent me.' He thought over that qualification for a moment and seemed to like it. 'But if it's the straight goods, I must conclude you are suffering some kind of breakdown.'

The slight Southern accent, as a matter of fact the whole bourbon and bayou conceit, had oozed away, Guerin noted. The bastard probably went to Oxford, he thought to himself. He had known agents who had so fallen in love with cover identities that they made them a permanent part of their life—these were tolerated as long as they were effective. 'You heard the girl, nobody believes us any more. Why should we trust each other?'

'You're talking about this supposed factionalism, aren't you? And you believe in it? As long as you've been around, you believe such a thing could actually happen ... in a national institution like the Firm? You're a goddamned idiot, Mercator. Furthermore, you're becoming counter-productive.'

Guerin stood easily, dangling his hands on the edge of the desk, every movement demonstrating good control of his body. 'Tell it to Fox! Tell it to my late friend. And his wife. And the two kids. Furthermore, I want to know who Homer is? And who sent him? I know you won't tell me, wouldn't if you could, but I'm going on record with the question. Because some day it will damn well have to be answered.'

Middlebrook shifted in his chair, restless, uneasy about how far the other man would go. His eyes, by great effort, he kept fixed on Guerin, who hovered over him. 'How would I know who he was? It's just a cover name in trip-licate, on blue, yellow and white forms, as far as I'm concerned. And it could be the President's Aunt Minnie in drag for all I care. Listen, it's none of your business any-way.'

'Not even if he was an assassin, Middlebrook, who was using the cover of the mission to get one of us?' It was easy to spot the leap to alarm in his opponent's eyes and that gave Guerin his straight easy line. 'I don't know who his primary target was, myself maybe, or the girl here ...' he hesitated only for a second ... 'but I think he killed Fox.'

The resident bolted out of his chair. 'Judas Priest! What the hell are you saying? You've lost your marbles.'

'If you're running a tape,' Guerin said evenly, 'and I assume you are, I want it clearly understood that my last comment was not official and I am making no such report to that effect.'

'You're violating every ... Jesus, Joseph and Mary ... This girl isn't one of us, you ought to know better than to say these things in front of her.' Middlebrook's own hands were flapping at his sides like wounded birds.

Guerin had gone too far not to finish it off now. 'I think she knows more about it than I do, and maybe you. Look, Middlebrook, I'm saying all this because I'm scared and I think the safest thing for me is a declaration of intent. I won't get involved in this factional madness. And that's what it is. So there's nothing left for me but to carry out my mission. What's done with that file, or even what's in it, is none of my business. But I'll get it, if she's telling the truth, and God help anyone in my way.'

Julia calmly lit a cigarette. It was the first time she had moved since the men had begun to quarrel.

Middlebrook, still standing, suddenly broke off the confrontation by telling them to spend another night at the SEFAS offices and to report back to him instantly when they had the file. Julia stood and walked out of the office, Guerin following without a word. Behind them there was a like silence. They went out through the building to the alley where the car with the Cuban driver was waiting. Guerin ordered the man to return to SEFAS without them.

12

They walked rapidly to get away from the building before anyone discovered they had not done as they had been told. Guerin thought there was a good chance the Cuban chauffeur would begin to worry and double back. He hailed a cab and told the driver to take MacArthur Causeway to Miami Beach. Julia went along without question.

'Apparently you do trust me,' he said, once they were settled back in the taxi.

She was staring out of the opposite window at nothing. 'Only compared to the others.'

'But you do trust me. I wonder why?'

'Don't make so much out of it.'

Eventually, after two changes of cabs, he took her back to the mainland and out to the University of Miami, where they walked around for hours. It was the most unlikely place he could think of.

Dinner was pizzas and a pitcher of watery beer at a student hangout where their racial mixture would not draw undue attention, because this was, after all, the South. Later, they found a tacky little out-of-the-way motel on the outskirts of Coral Gables. Julia insisted upon her own room, saying that her life in Cuba had made privacy important to her. Guerin trusted her in this; he had to—if he couldn't he knew he was finished anyway.

They were both subdued on the way to Miami International Airport the next morning, but Guerin felt his spirits climbing the moment he was out of the cab in front of the terminal. Initially, it could have been as simple as his love of everything having to do with airlines and flying; he had often thought about getting a licence himself but had never been in one place long enough. Julia seemed to pick up, too, once they were inside. Watching her obliquely, he registered the *élan* creeping back into her eyes and walk, and began to experience renewed hope that maybe they were only minutes away from having the papers in their hands. Certainly Julia looked as though she believed it. There was a mechanized pathway out to the boarding areas but it moved too slowly for them this morning and they walked.

Going out through the tunnel, she asked, 'Are we very early?'

'Not too bad, twenty minutes or so. Will you tell me now who we're meeting?'

'A man who works for the Swiss Embassy in Havana. His name is Peter Zahner.'

'A friend?'

She nodded affirmatively. He watched her stride, thinking that a week ago in Cuba it had probably been the sensuous side-to-side of tropical women, and now, even in sub-tropical America, it was the confident, determined carriage of a suburban matron. He was not sure if he liked that or not.

'Your lover?' he asked, keeping his voice ordinary.

She glanced at him quizzically. 'Oh, yes,' she said, 'one of the many.'

'Sorry.'

'Sometimes, for a man your age and especially in your profession, you're very childish.'

'I just wanted to know why he took such chances for you.'

'That's why. Anyway, he has diplomatic immunity, so it's very easy.'

'Can you trust him?'

'I would like a cup of coffee, if we have time.'

As it turned out, they did not. The plane from Mexico City, where Zahner would have had to have gone to make connections for the United States, came in several minutes early and Guerin and Julia had to hurry away from the coffee shop to be at the railing when the first passengers appeared. She was nervous now and beyond hiding it. Guerin scanned each face as it came through, although he could do no more than look for a recognizable type since he had never seen a picture of Zahner. Passenger after passenger bustled out of the tunnel into the waiting crowd to be swallowed by hungering relatives or friends or lost in the minutia of the disembarkation routine. Guerin caught himself moistening his lips and put a stop to it.

'Julia!' called a man with a German raincoat over his shoulders. Guerin's gaze shifted to him almost imperceptibly. On the short side, with a tanned face above a blue-tinged, two-a-day-beard. Forty to fifty. Possible Slav, but more likely Middle European. Well-dressed, brisk, almost arrogant walk, thinning hair brushed mostly forward. Looked to be wearing a waist cincher. He hoped this would not be Julia's lover.

By tacit agreement they had separated themselves at the railing. Guerin, however, had been careful to place himself close enough to the girl to be able to overhear anything said to her. He already knew from a single furtive glance that she was startled and perhaps frightened by the appearance of this particular man.

'Emile!' she called him. And then Guerin heard her ask, 'Where is he?' in a lost, desperate, child's voice.

The man's reply, accompanied by a chuckle he seemed to think winning, was spoken so softly it was impossible for Guerin to get any more than its drift. Still smiling, he removed an envelope from inside his suit coat and handed it to Julia, who seemed almost inclined to reject it—she held it out in front of her as though it was something alive and possibly venomous. The man appeared to be amused by her reaction. He tipped his hat, said something in the way of a goodbye, and quickly disappeared into the crowds headed for the front of the terminal.

For an instant, Guerin was tempted to follow him, but he decided against it. Once he knew who the man was it would not be difficult to find him, and everything about Julia told him that she was pathetically vulnerable now. With fingers trembling noticeably, she tore open the letter and read it. Guerin waited because it was easier to interpret a performance at a distance. The life drained from her face and he was convinced; there were not many actors who could control their metabolism. He went over to support her.

The letter was crumpled and lying on the floor by the time he reached her side. Picking it up, he read it to himself:

My Dear Julia,

Emile has kindly consented to deliver this on his way to Washington, since I will assuredly, by the time you read it, be comfortably situated at home. That is, in Zurich. I have been granted a month's holiday before my next posting. During that time perhaps I shall hear from you ... or your friends.

You know, my dear, it was you who always maintained we must never trust anyone in this sordid world. Regrettably, you were correct. Once the contents of your little gift packet were known to me, I could scarcely fail to recognize the opportunity which rarely comes to any man. Please don't judge me too harshly.

Fondly,

Peter.

'Pompous bastard!' Julia exploded, looking in the direction Peter's surrogate had gone.

'Did he always talk like this?' Guerin could not entirely repress a grin.

She turned on him angrily. 'Do you think I could have stood him if he did?'

'No, it's written for us,' he allowed. 'And possibly the competition.'

'What do you mean?'

People surged around them, the noise of greetings, kisses, complaints, businessmen, priests, sailors, coming, going and waiting: but they were an island, isolated by the seriousness of their concerns in the midst of a chaotic normality. Awkward as it was, Guerin felt no desire to move, to go anywhere. 'It's going to be lousy.' He grimaced. 'We're beginning all over.'

'He's blackmailing you, isn't he?'

Guerin nodded.

'Is there a chance your people will go and kill him for it?'

'I don't know,' he told her with a shrug, 'that's the least of my concerns.'

'It's not the least of mine,' she said.

As they came out of the terminal, Guerin, who was guiding Julia gently by the arm, felt her tense-up. He looked aside at her, and then followed her gaze to a man entering a taxi at the curb. A Latin. 'What is it?'

She stopped and stared after the departing cab for a moment, and he waited patiently beside her. 'That man who got into that cab,' she said finally, 'I think I knew him. From Cuba.'

He didn't know whether to believe her or not. 'Who do you think it was?'

'I only saw the back of his head. It looked like an officer of the G-2. We met on only one occasion, more than a year ago. My girl-friend introduced us, but he was a little sinister for my taste.' She looked at Guerin crossly. 'Don't smile! Anyway, I think his name was Cespedes.'

'What does he have to do with our problems?'

'Nothing that I know of.'

'I think maybe you're wound a little tight. They don't export officers as illegals, generally. They can depend on sympathizers. Or the Russians. And if he's that well-known they'll pick him up pretty quick anyway.'

She eased her arm free of his grip. 'Look, he can blow up Washington, for all I care, as long as I'm not in it.'

Guerin suspected now that she had seen what she had said she had, although he did not know what it implied. Frowning, he decided it was perhaps one more good reason to act on his own.

They took a taxicab into downtown Miami and purchased some odds and ends, things they needed for day to day living, from a department store, then boarded a bus at a suburban terminal bound for Washington. Julia again

129

went along without question, and Guerin felt relatively secure about it as a gambit, because nobody at the Firm ever took a bus.

13

The decisive interrogation of Julia Fernandez-Estrellita took place three days after her arrival in Washington; that, together with the fact that it was carried on at the highest level, indicated to Guerin the measure of concern felt by the hierarchy of the Firm about the missing file. It was held in the enormous third floor office of the Deputy Director of Plans, although the man himself was absent, purportedly on a tour of inspection of Southeast Asia. In his place was the Executive Assistant to the DDP, a pudgy, bespectacled man with a professorial air named Callison. Also present were Guerin, Hammerle, a man Guerin knew to be a staff psychologist, Byrd, and a fifth man he suspected of being from the Bureau, but who remained anonymous.

'Did you read the file while it was in your hands, Miss Fernandez?' It was Callison who had asked, even as he circled to his chair behind the outsized kidney-shaped plateau of a desk.

'Of course not,' Julia replied coolly. 'I had definite instructions from my support officer not to.'

'Where do you think he got instructions from?'

'I was told it was Virgil, the resident in Key West.'

'And his instructions?'

'How should I know?'

Guerin gazed out of the mammoth window. One of the deer came from the woods in the distance and stared at the building. Julia, well ... she was being Julia, lying with dignity, and conceit, but of course they knew it. A bad and good beginning, bad for content, good for style. He admired her, she was not intimidated even here.

'Why,' Callison went on in a low key, 'did you decide to disobey orders?'

Julia allowed herself to smile. 'I disobeyed so many, you'll have to be more specific.'

'Your reasons for demanding to be removed from the island with the papers were transmitted to us at the time, and to some extent we were sympathetic to the request. Motivational exhaustion, particularly in personnel operating clandestinely as you were, is a phenomenon we deal with here every day, and it's not something to which we ascribe blame ordinarily. On the other hand, the way you went about it was very close to blackmail.' He managed to make it sound like a reprimand from a kindly school counsellor.

'It was blackmail,' she agreed. 'I thought that since I was kept there by blackmail it was only fair I get out the same way.'

There was a silence which the psychologist, Byrd, felt obligated to fill. 'I'll say one thing for Miss Fernandez, she certainly didn't come here as a penitent.' He smiled around, but no one joined him.

Julia agreed that she had not.

'Miss Fernandez, why did you fail to bring out the papers the way you had promised,' the assistant DDP went on, '*after* we acceded to your "request" to leave your post?'

'I don't understand,' Julia said evenly. She was sitting up very primly with her hands clasped in her lap like any well-poised clubwoman waiting to address a luncheon gathering. 'I've been asked these same questions over and over again during the last couple of days. You must have the record there on your desk. If I was lying I wouldn't change my answers now, would I? Unless you put matches under my fingernails or something.'

Callison smiled sweetly. 'I'm afraid I'll have to disappoint you in that respect. We try never to torture nice young ladies here.' He pulled a battered, leather-jacketed pipe out of his equally venerable tweed jacket and concentrated on filling it.

'We're all family men here, Miss Fernandez,' the psychologist assured her, and even the dour man from the Bureau looked to see if he was kidding. Apparently he was not. 'If they told you anything of that sort in Cuba they were lying.'

So much, Guerin thought, for sorting out the cold war.

'Please answer Mr Callison's questions,' Hammerle insisted, putting just enough edge on it to bring them back to the real world.

'What will happen if I don't?'

Silence again. Guerin was sitting to one side and behind Julia, and it was difficult to read her face. Callison studied the file in front of him. The psychologist whistled soundlessly. The Bureau's man seemed scornful of the proceedings, as though he was sure they could do it better over at their house. Whatever Julia's game was, Guerin had no inkling of it. They had been separated most of the time since their arrival, but it was unlikely she would have discussed her intentions with him anyway. And he felt basically the same, there were many things he was not prepared to tell her even if it might benefit her, and, given some sort of Draconian choice, he was quite prepared to throw her to whatever wolves were extant rather than endanger for a single moment his career and its attendant benefits.

Still, there was an excitement about her which was something far more than sexual. She surprised him constantly, having no right, really, to be as bright and sophisticated as she was: like now, when a ghetto-raised black chicana girl with a year of college sat up in front of the power elite of the American system and insisted upon dictating the terms of her own treatment. Along that line of thought, Guerin shifted his gaze to the battered, unsubstantial clothes she had brought with her from Cuba, and felt himself slipping dangerously close to sentimentality.

'Why did you refuse to take a lie detector test yesterday?' the Bureau man asked abruptly.

Julia made a gesture of indifference. 'I just don't like the idea. And besides, I'm not a regular employee, I've never signed your oaths or anything of that sort, so I don't think you have the right to ask me.'

Hammerle told her she was running the risk of losing all of her pay for the years of service to the Firm, or, as he put it, to her country. It had, as was customary he reminded, been deposited for her regularly in a bank in the United States, since there was no question of her receiving it while still in Cuba. Julia asked if they could do that to her? Hammerle replied never mind whether it was legal or ethical, the only pertinent question was how could she prevent them from doing it?

'Forgive me if I repeat myself,' said Callison mildly, 'but why did you refuse to bring the papers out with you?'

Julia sighed. 'I didn't trust you. When you live in secrecy for a long time and have to do things without ever knowing why you are doing them, or even for whom, then you don't trust so easily after a while. I was afraid you would take the papers and leave me there. Maybe dead. I wouldn't be the first one.'

Callison had nothing but contempt for that line of reasoning, or at least he worked at conveying that response, imploring the ceiling, pressing his fingertips against one another and turning partially away, then back again. 'Ridiculous. Your life was in our hands for years. Why should you think we would do such a thing. We're not the communists you know.'

'Mr Callison, if you expect me to respect you and tell

the truth, then you shouldn't patronize me. You aren't a communist, so far as I know, but neither am I a stupid woman.'

Everyone waited for a cue from Callison—it came in the form of a chuckle. 'No wonder you lasted so long in the Ministry; you're a resourceful girl and you don't trust anyone. And quite rightly. I could be one of them, couldn't I? I will try to treat you with more respect, Miss Fernandez.'

'Thank you.' She continued to look at ease with herself.

'Now if you will only please tell us why you gave vitally important papers to this Zahner chap. Or why you trusted him more than us?'

'Peter is a man completely without politics . . .'

'Or morals,' Hammerle put in.

The slightest movement of Julia's head indicated to Guerin that she knew that was intended to include her. 'I don't want to argue philosophy with you,' she said to Hammerle, 'but I trust a man without morals more than a man with politics. Take yourself, if I were to spend a few hours in your company I would know a lot about your morals no matter how you tried to disguise them, but I wouldn't have any idea whether or not you were a member of the "Element".'

Another silence fell, which drowned all the others by comparison. Julia turned and looked, for the first time, at Guerin. Her face was totally without expression, she merely looked at him. He felt his stomach tighten.

Callison sucked on his dry pipe and asked coldly, 'What precisely is the "Element"?'

Julia looked at Hammerle and formed her words carefully. 'Or the "Bourse".'

'What,' Callison repeated in the same steady tone, 'is the "Element"?'

'I thought you said we were going to be honest with each other.'

Callison did not ask a third time. Hammerle demanded to know: 'Did Mr Guerin tell you about that?'

'No, it was well known to everyone in the underground. Your people who came and went, they told us.'

'Exactly what did they tell you?' the psychologist wanted to know.

'You know, that you were having a civil war, hurting and even killing each other whenever you could, a right and left wing. I can never remember which is which because I'm not political myself.' She aimed that patent sarcasm at Hammerle again.

'And Mr Guerin never once mentioned this supposed factionalism?'

'Only when I brought it up—he answered me. He was like you, he pretended there was no such thing.'

'Did he at any time accuse the man on the boat coming back, called Homer, of being involved in this so-called "Element"?' the man from the Bureau asked.

Guerin looked at him, in appearance he was like most of the Bureau's agents: grey all over, not too tall (the Director of that organization was notoriously short), narrow flowered tie with monochromatic colours (the Director hated striped or wide ties, buttoned down or large shirt collars and other sartorial accoutrements he associated with the products of Eastern schools), looked, on the whole, less than brilliant, but then the Director valued loyalty, honesty, and persistence far more than intelligence, which he somehow thought of as his enemy, perhaps for the same causal relationship that had formed his attitudes about tall men.

'I don't remember him saying that, although he didn't seem to trust him. This man Homer, incidentally, tried to find out from me about the papers I was bringing.' The interrogators exchanged looks. 'Mr Guerin also told me that he had insisted on coming ashore to pick me up when he was not supposed to. And that was the sort of thing I was afraid of in the first place, I might add.'

'Why,' Hammerle demanded, turning to Guerin, 'did you distrust a member of your own component, so much that you disobeyed orders and went on to the island yourself?'

Guerin, like Julia, had been asked these or related questions continuously for the last two days; unlike her, he felt no desire to point that out to these gentlemen.

'Sanford was a friend of mine. I'd always known him to be a stable, responsible man and a good agent. But he came on this mission under the impression that one of these supposed factions was trying to kill him.'

The psychologist broke in, sounding depressingly clinical, 'Did he say how he knew that? What proof he had? How long he had felt this way?'

'No, and I was sceptical at first, but then a series of things began to look wrong. Beginning, actually, when I met Sandy the night before I left Washington. He said he would be followed to the restaurant, and he was.' He turned to the Bureau man. 'One of your people.'

'What makes you think so?' the accused asked sharply.

'It's one of the first things we learn.'

Callison, no doubt sensing that inter-service rivalry was about to consume their attention, waved irritably for Guerin to go on.

'Sandy seemed to feel I would be compromised simply for having known him. And then I was followed again when I was in Miami.'

The psychologist was going to break in again, but Callison preferred to hear Guerin.

'When Homer joined our component he was openly insubordinate. He claimed to have his own orders—nothing in writing—telling him to go ashore as bodyguard to the agent, in this case Sandy, who was going in after Miss Fernandez. He was a pretty hard-nosed type, Homer, and I had to deal with him accordingly. You'll no doubt find something about that in his report. Anyway, Sandy thought

Homer represented the people who wanted to eliminate him, and of course he was sophisticated enough to know that the perfect situation, from a theoretical assassin's point of view, would be on Hostile territory while in the midst of performing a mission. I mean, it's almost standard, isn't it?' He knew as soon as he had said it that he should not have added that last qualification.

But if his interrogators thought so, they gave no indication. The other four men were universally glum, and a couple of them, he thought, openly disapproving. Under the circumstances he could hardly expect otherwise. He did not dare look at Julia during all this. Callison asked him, 'So you went ashore yourself simply to protect your friend?'

Guerin saw that an affirmative answer would mean the end of his career. Would, in fact, be considered in this world a kind of treason. He hoped his voice carried conviction. 'No, sir, of course not. I went ashore as the best way to ensure the success of the mission. To protect the agent I had been sent to bring out.' He glanced at Hammerle. 'I had been told that it was extremely important. Later, on Manna Key and with the resident in Miami, my actions were intended, as they have always been, to carry out to the best of my judgment the assignment I had been given. As it turned out, I lost both my friend and the thing I had been sent to get, but I would have to do it exactly the same way again.'

'I see,' Callison murmured mechanically, staring out the big picture window. Guerin followed his line of sight. The deer had gone back into the trees. Large grey clouds were forming on the horizon, assuming shapes, being blown forward by the wind bringing the threat of rain, although, had it not been so early in the year, it might easily have been snow. Guerin had told it all, except that both Hammerle and the Miami resident had said things about the girl who was sitting with them now that had made him consider whether or not her life might also be in danger. He could not bring that up.

Guerin suddenly started in again. 'As you know, I've expressed an opinion about Sanford's death that ...'

Callison did not let him finish the sentence. In a voice that carried an almost Prussian severity he cut in: 'I'd rather you didn't express it now.'

Guerin gave it up as much out of surprise as obedience. Could it be that the others, even Hammerle, had not read his report? Or was it only because the Bureau man was there? He saw them look at Callison, all three, and decided that he had been right the first time. He felt cold; it would be unbearable if Sandy's murder were swallowed up in the bureaucratic silence, as so many had been.

Callison seemed to have made a decision, he stood up abruptly. 'That's enough for now, I want to think about some of these things. If we have more questions I'll call you back in. If we don't, a decision will be made before tomorrow as to how we can proceed on this matter. In the meantime,' and he smiled almost paternally, 'you have the good fortune to be responsible for Miss Fernandez, Mr Guerin.'

Guerin was grateful; he was desperately anxious to get out of that office. They said a well-modulated, almost formal set of goodbyes, however, and left as though they could hardly bear to part from one another. Guerin took Julia's arm and steered her through the long, antiseptic, tiled halls with their glaucous lighting, past the countless checkpoints and guards, and it was several moments before he spoke. 'Pretty damned cheeky in there, weren't you? What made you decide to give them a hard time? I mean Middlebrook is one thing ...'

Julia still seemed pleased with herself. He thought she looked like a kid who had got away with sassing the principal, and it irritated him, he wanted to cut her down to size, to remind her that in the real world people's lives were sometimes forfeit. 'I learned a long time ago with men, all men,' she told him, 'that they believe your lies better when you are aggressive with them, when you keep them on the defensive.'

'Oh,' was all he said.

'What do you mean, "oh"?'

Guerin was not up to playing games after the last few days. They left the building and headed for the parking lot. 'Don't you think they know when you're lying and when you're not?' His voice was hard.

She changed mood immediately. 'Oh, Stephen, I'm so goddamned tired of all this.'

'They don't care,' he told her.

As they drove away towards Washington, he began to wonder what else he might do with his life.

14

Guerin took the opportunity to go over to Georgetown and see Sandy's family, hoping every mile of the way that the boys would be elsewhere and it would only be the widow there. Besides the usual reasons, he had cause to dread it because it was just possible that she had not yet been notified of Sandy's death. The Firm was sometimes less than prompt about that sort of thing for a variety of reasons, mostly having to do with security. For his own security reasons he had not been able to call ahead to see if she knew. He had not even asked the company for permission to go.

They lived in a block of Georgian-styled duplexes on a street full of soft feathery trees. Everything substantial, neat, well-ordered, where even death would have to feel itself an intruder. He had not expected a black wreath or anything of that sort, but somehow the placid normality of the place bothered him: flowers in the windowboxes, a toy car and football on the front lawn, the afternoon paper waiting to be taken in. He parked at the kerb and dragged himself up to the door. He rang and, while waiting for it to be answered, tried a variety of masks. Ideally it would be one that combined sorrow without gloom and good humour without callousness. Glancing at the brass door fixtures and the carriage lamp beside it, he caught himself wondering how Sandy could afford this place, then he remembered that something in Helen's background had made her proficient in two or three oriental languages, so she often worked as a highly paid translator for several corporations and government bureaus—everywhere in Washington but the Firm, where they had a rule against employing relatives of employees.

Just as the door opened, Sandy's youngest, Mark, who was four, trundled around the side of the building and looked at him. Guerin tried to be very hearty but it turned out to be unnecessary, because the boy obviously did not remember him. How long had it been? Helen greeted him and shooed her son around to the back in the same sweeping, efficient action. She was tearless and managed a fragment of a smile, but Guerin could see that he would be spared anything catastrophic. He followed her into the living room and waited while she opened the blinds, sitting only when invited.

'I somehow never thought of you as a sentimental man, Stephen. This is really awfully considerate of you.' There was nothing to say to that, he only gestured. 'Did you ask the Firm if it was all right to come out here?' Before he could answer, she had a somewhat different thought. 'Or did they send you?'

Guerin saw trouble coming in the qualification. 'No,' he said, 'they don't know I'm here.'

'Aren't you apt to get in trouble?'

'I doubt it.'

'Do you want a drink?'

'No, thank you.' He could have used it emotionally, or just as something to occupy his hands, but he did not want to be around long enough to consume it. 'I'm damned sorry, Helen. I don't know what else to say, but I really am ... damned sorry ...'

She flicked on that furtive, fragile smile. 'Of course. Everyone is. Especially me. And the boys. I've sent Larry to my parents, Mark is too young to really understand, and in fact I haven't even tried to tell him yet. Of course we've lived on the brink around here for a long time, so you can see we're all holding up nicely.'

She did not look as though she was; looked, in fact, as if she might burst into tears at any moment. 'I'll have the drink if you will,' Guerin said, to brake her descent. Also, she had been sitting on the couch opposite, with her legs curled up underneath her the way women do, and he had caught himself noticing those legs, which was unthinkable under the circumstances and made him very uneasy with himself.

She went to an expensive-looking antique secretary and extracted a bottle of Scotch and two glasses. Holding it up in demonstration, she commented, 'I hope you don't think I've gotten on this since my widowhood, but I have had a couple. Stephen, you were with him, weren't you?'

He looked up, surprised, and she put the glass in his hand. 'How did you know that?'

'Nothing sinister. I just put together a couple of facts —Sandy told me he had run into you at the plant, but you were being sent out, then he was sent out, and now here you are so soon after—with my woman's intuition ... whatever the hell that is.' She tossed down the liquor with something like disdain for its effect.

'I was with him on the mission, but not at the moment

when he was killed. It was a Cuban affair. Do you want to hear the details?'

She thought it over. 'No,' she decided, 'I don't. And you'd only get in trouble, anyway.' Making a hopeless gesture with long patrician hands, she added, 'What good would it do us, what possible good?'

The plaintive quality in her voice wrenched at Guerin's heart in a way he had dreaded since the first moment he had decided to come. 'Are you going to have some kind of service?' he asked, largely to fill the silence.

It was either distinctly the right or wrong thing to say, because Helen's head came up and her eyes took on a certain glint. 'No, I don't think so. Sandy didn't practice his religion. And besides, the Firm wouldn't like it, would they?'

It was a leading question, Guerin knew that. Still, he gave her the lead. 'I'm sure they wouldn't care. It's none of their business.'

She made a brittle sound like a laugh. 'The man who brought me the news, his name was Dunphy or something like that, said that he hoped if we did have a service, it would be small and private and I would give the cover story—not that he told me the real one—but that I would tell the appropriate lies to the priest or rabbi or whatever we had. He didn't seem to know what people had at a funeral.'

'They only know about the Russian Orthodox Church at the Firm.' He hoped that might sound blandly witty.

'He told me,' she went on, 'that since there was no body anyway, I probably wouldn't want to go through the useless strain of such a ceremony.'

'Maybe he's right.'

'And he suggested, oh very subtly and politely—you're all such gentlemen—but he thought that it would be very unfortunate if there was a service and anything leaked out to the press. You remember, don't you Stephen, the boy

142

down in North Carolina whose relatives gave all the interviews after a friend showed up at his funeral and told them in strictest confidence what had really happened to their son. Well, the Firm never got over that, it seems, at least from what Mr Dunphy said.'

Guerin was feeling increasingly miserable, but he could not allow himself to become defensive. 'You know they make a lot of threats, Helen, they're in that business. But you're sophisticated enough to handle it.'

'Oh? How do I handle it if the pension cheques stop coming from that mysterious trust fund in Chicago or wherever the hell it is—I don't know because I haven't got one yet. But what do I do, Stephen? Sue them or him or it? Get a lawyer and say that my husband gave twelve years to a dangerous job that got him killed and now they won't even help raise his children. I'd have trouble convincing that lawyer that I ever even had a husband, because he was in clandestine and as far as this country is concerned, the one he served, he didn't exist. An "unperson", I think you call them at work, don't you?'

Guerin finished his drink quickly. 'I'll try to find out, and influence whatever and whoever I can.'

A lot of the tensile quality went out of her body and the voice grew dispirited. 'What for? I said we didn't want a religious ceremony anyway.' She looked out the window behind the couch, where the shape of her youngest son crossed and recrossed in play. 'In future we'll just do as you people say, I suppose. Not very much to ask. The allowance is generous, after all, and I can work.'

The conflict, the conversation as a whole, ran down after that. Guerin stayed long enough to demonstrate, to himself at least, that he was not offended by anything untoward said about the Firm, and went so far as to assure Helen, while hating the necessity to do so, that he would not convey any of her bitterness to the people who were in a position to hurt her. Personally, he thought she had exaggerated things.

He hesitated at the door on the way out and asked: 'Helen, did Sandy ever mention the "Bourse"?'

'What do you mean—the French stock exchange?'

He laughed self-consciously. 'No, no, something else, an organization. I believe it got that name because they're men who are supposed to be willing to do business, so to speak. Anyway that's the story.'

'No, he didn't. And now he never will. We're through with all that here. Goodbye, Stephen.'

He believed her. It was easy, because he was anxious to get away.

It was a glorious day, fragrant and sunny with the air just beginning to slip towards an autumnal crispness. On the way back to Washington he decided to feel better through an act of will. Not that he had any objective reason to; Julia had suddenly been moved somewhere out of touch, and even his own future was somewhat in doubt. No one could or would give him any idea when he might expect to hear the conclusions drawn from their interrogations. In fact, he did not know to whom or what section he was assigned, and therefore had difficulty determining where he might expect to receive answers from whenever they were forthcoming.

Worst of all had been the realization that came home to him at the instant Mark had failed to identify him: Sandy and he had liked each other but they had not been close friends. They had met four years before while both were attached to the Department of Disaster Evaluation, sorting out the consequences when an agent or whole component was surfaced somewhere and recommending defensive measures, and during that period they would occasionally go out for a drink after work. He had been out to Sandy's for dinner on perhaps a half dozen occasions, bought presents for the children's birthdays, but generally without being there to see them receive them. Once, when he had been going with Phyllis, they had, in effect, double-dated. All very intramural, the way it always was in the Firm, but how could he have thought of this as a deep and close friendship?

There was one small thing he could find to feel good about; Helen had not yet at the time of his visit been advised about the non-medal Sandy would receive. Thank God he had not mentioned that.

15

Shortly before noon of the next day, Guerin, who had gone home to his own apartment, was summoned to the plant and told to see a man named Papasian, a sad-eyed little Armenian from Beirut who looked like an Arab rug-pedlar but spoke impeccable English and had a good reputation all through the Atlantic sectors. Papasian was crisp and businesslike. Before Guerin was fully seated he was told that he would be allowed to complete his mission; he was being sent to Switzerland to bargain for the file with the blackmailer, Zahner.

Guerin, amazed, asked if that meant that Julia's story was believed? The Armenian replied that 'believed' might semantically be a bit strong, but it was, for the moment at least, acknowledged as a basis for procedure. He was to report to Transportation, where he would be given two tickets on a commercial airline flight for Berne, Switzerland; further instructions would be waiting for him in the hands of the resident at the embassy.

'Two tickets, you said. Who's coming with me?'

Papasian was studying the itinerary on his desk. 'The girl,' he said. 'She knows the chap, after all.'

Guerin returned to his apartment within the hour, packed a single suitcase and was driven by another agent to the Woman's Army barracks outside Washington, where Julia had been secreted for the night under guard, and then on to Dulles International. As the sun set they rose up and flew out over the black brooding swells of the Atlantic.

It being a covert mission, there was no one to meet them when they arrived at the airport in Berne. They checked into a small pension in a not very fashionable quarter of the town, since State was known to pay poorly and he was posing as a lower echelon employee of that organization. Julia, who said she had never been to Europe, thought it was beautiful, however. Modest as it was, there remained the failing fall flowers in the red window boxes, a bright blue roof, big high-ceilinged rooms with marble washbasins and full of handsome antique furniture; and of course the Swiss hosteliers, with their age-old indifference once financial matters were resolved, took no notice of Julia's colour.

She mentioned it to Guerin when he came down to her room to take her to the embassy. 'Why should they?' he asked.

'You haven't known many black people, have you?'

'No, I suppose not. There are a few in the company, of course.'

'There are a few in Washington, about eighty per cent of the population,' she reminded him, as she paused at the mirror to finish her makeup.

Guerin was giving the room a cursory examination for signs of bugging. 'Sure, but those, as I think you know very well, are invisible to anyone who lives like I do.'

She turned and looked at him. 'They're free in Cuba now. Completely free.'

Guerin felt a twinge of uneasiness. 'I don't know why the hell you're telling me that. Or why now? But I think you should keep in mind the fact that I didn't pick this hotel. The reservations were made for us by the Firm.'

'I don't care if they hear me. Come on.'

Because of the difference in their position, Julia was asked to remain outside while Guerin, an officer, was briefed by the Swiss resident, a man named Drury, in his bedroom at the embassy. There was nothing in the content that he would not tell Julia within a few minutes after leaving the place, but he endured while at the same time conscious of the fact that procedures he used to take for granted were increasingly a source of irritation, or something worse—despair.

At the conclusion of the briefing, most of which had to do with Swiss police practices and attitudes, it was suggested that Guerin pick up the phone on the bedside table beside him and contact Zahner.

'I think it makes more sense to have the Fernandez girl talk to him. She knows him, his voice, his psychology. I presume that's why she was sent here in the first place.'

The resident, an older man who seemed almost phlegmatic to Guerin, nodded agreeably and led him to an office on the ground floor where Julia joined them. A German-speaking secretary came in to place the call, taking the number from a piece of paper given her by the resident.

'How do you know he'll be there?' the agent asked.

The resident slumped into a French Provincial chair that, Guerin estimated, must have cost two hundred American dollars. He looked like he might have been a worn-out cop of some kind, because he was dumpy and baggy and did not suit the chair. 'We've had a close watch on him for several days. He's not going anywhere, he's waiting for you. Or them.'

The ring was audible in the room as the secretary held up the phone and looked around for instructions. Guerin pointed to Julia, who took it gingerly. Watching her, he measured the increase of nervous intensity in her hands and eyes and lips, and felt something akin to jealousy. It turned out that Zahner had put his calls through an answering service but the woman on the other end spoke English well enough for Julia to convey her intent and her name. That took a few more minutes, during which the resident leaned forward lazily to punch up a tape recorder. At last a male voice came on the line. It was not necessary for Guerin to wait for verbal confirmation that this was Zahner—Julia stiffened appreciably.

'Julia, is that really you?'

'Yes, Peter, it's me.'

'I cannot believe it, I never thought they would send you.'

'No, I don't imagine you did.' She was holding the receiver a tiny distance from her ear, so that the two men might listen. That made Guerin feel a little better, although he was embarrassed by the feeling.

A smile came into Zahner's voice in recognition of her sarcasm. 'Oh, my poor darling, how you must hate me. But try to understand, such an opportunity comes to a man so seldom, if ever, in a lifetime.' He laughed, no doubt with what he felt was charm. And yet Julia responded to it with a near-smile of her own. Guerin consoled himself that a woman will almost always feel at least something from the gaiety of an ex-lover, even when it's turned against her. 'Listen, you know, you never should have trusted me. Why did you, Julia? You're not a trusting woman. And you're certainly not stupid. I should think with your background ...' She jammed the receiver tight against her ear, cutting off the sound. Guerin winced at the obviousness of it; she knew, of course, that it was being recorded, but it had been instinctual.

'Peter,' she cut in anxiously, 'please don't waste our time with this silliness. It's in your interest as well as ours to finish off this thing quickly. Where can we meet you?'

She was holding the phone out again and Guerin could hear Zahner laugh when he said, 'Are you afraid someone will hurt me, Julia? Perhaps you are still fond of me, after all.' There was an hysterical quality in the man's voice; Peter was terrified, in over his head, and it would be important to get to him as soon as possible.

'Peter,' Julia said, with impressive coldness, 'I do have some pleasant memories of you, but as you know I live only in the present, and right now there is nothing in the world I would like better than to watch somebody strangle you very slowly with a piano wire. And to see you beg for mercy so I could laugh my goddamn head off. That's how I feel now—do I make myself clear?'

Guerin glanced at the resident. He might have been a little surprised, but he seemed to be enjoying it.

Zahner must have been impressed, too, because after that he got down to business and named a garden restaurant on the Zurich lakeshore and a time late on the following day. His only stipulation was that she come alone. Guerin shook his head 'no' vigorously.

'I'm sorry,' she said on the phone, 'but that's impossible. There will be another man with me, or no deal at all.'

Zahner grumbled but Guerin could tell that he was incapable of putting up any real resistance at this point. Julia hung up and at the resident's suggestion they went back to their pension and checked out. Guerin took with him a draft on a Swiss bank for two hundred and fifty thousand dollars. Within two hours they were on an electric train for Zurich.

That cold autumn night in the Canton of Zurich, with the wars suspended for the few brief hours of darkness, Guerin and Julia slept together. It was the first, and would be the only time, but it was a memorable love-making and Guerin thought it might actually imply love. He had not dealt with love since his adolescence, but he had the idea that it must be like this. Lying and staring at the dawn as it crept across the ceiling he suddenly remembered that it was his thirty-sixth birthday. He tried to remember other birthdays, his last birthday, but ordinarily they went by without notice and there was nothing to mark any of them all the way back to the twelfth, when his mother had asked his father for a divorce, and later in that same day relented.

He reached over to pull back the comforter in order to see her against the vanilla sheets, a contrast that thrilled him aesthetically as well as erotically. The light that set it off was the silvery grey of early morning filtered through a leaded window. He did not want to think about the coming day, or even the mission in general, but let his mind idle with the dust that floated about in the shafts of light. Was it that they used different components for the glass in Switzerland, or simply the properties of clear mountain air? It was true that light was often peculiar to a particular place and time; the lavender sky around Paris at twilight was like no other in the world surely—even an amateur could see it. Perhaps he would take up his painting again when this was over. But he would stay with the Firm no matter what—that was not a negotiable change, either with Julia, or himself, or the people who were factionalizing it for whatever insane ideological purposes. Of course he might have to take a rest when the mission was over, try to get the neuroses under control before he was found out. When they sacked you at the Firm it was irrevocable, and the only formality required was the Director's name on a piece of paper. Twenty years of service could be totally obliterated with the regurgitation of a fortran card bearing your name into a certain basket.

The girl stirred and whimpered. She was obviously cold from his having pulled back the covers, and now she drew up her legs to assume the fetal position for warmth. It was amazing, Guerin thought, how lovely she was in that ungainly attitude which would have done damage to any other girl he had ever known. He touched her thigh gently and she shivered; after that he placed the cover over her again. For an unknown reason his imagination imbued that insignificant gesture with a morbid finality, a prescience, the feeling that he was drawing a veil between himself and any hope for a natural life. He got out of bed, partially dressed, and went to stare out the window at the snow-rumpled mountains in the far distance. His bare feet and chest were rigid with cold and yet he was sweating. No, no good, he murmured to himself; he was cracking like the Firm, like the parent, like father like son, not in a clean straight line but fragmenting into a thousand small and crooked ones, like, or so he suspected, the larger world outside the Firm that nurtured it and provided its reason for being.

Sometimes he wondered about his isolation from the outside; was it possible that if he were free to discuss the general interest with ordinary people he would find that the Firm was an anachronism, or unwanted, or superfluous, or did not even exist for them. In the last couple of years he had noticed that he was most comfortable when assuming a cover, and the more outrageous the pose the more he felt at home with it, but whenever he tried to behave naturally and openly with people, then he suffered the greatest anxiety. A milk truck entered the narrow deserted street beneath his window and cruised to a stop. The driver emerged whistling and went into a building to make a delivery. An ordinary man doing commonplace things. Guerin sighed enviously, and, he knew, hypocritically.

'You look miserable, Stephen. Come back to bed.'

Her voice startled him, as much for its blunt tactile quality under the circumstances as the surprise. But he should have known; Julia would not be one to linger about coming awake, even after love-making; she would speak directly, honestly and to the point. He went over and sat on the edge of the bed staring across the room.

'Julia, I want to know what's in the papers.'

She gave a small staccato laugh, and for a moment he thought she would be angry. 'You are suddenly very direct, aren't you?' she said. 'First we make love, then you are paid.'

'I would hope you know better than that. Don't you?'

'Are you going to tell me, because I've slept with you, that now I should see the real man, that you've stopped being what you are?' She put her hand on his back and began to massage it thoughtfully.

'Will you tell me?'

'You've waited a long time to ask.'

'I know. But I feel like questioning everything.'

'All right,' she said, sitting up abruptly to light a cigarette. He had to wait through a long contemplative inhalation. 'There were a lot of papers and I didn't take the time to study them, or maybe I was just compromising with my conscience by only glancing at them ...' She paused and looked around at him. 'You don't believe that? Anyway, they dealt with the assassination of Kennedy.' He was grateful that she did not pause for effect. 'In fact, the one, which was signed by Che Guevara and countersigned by Dorticos and Rao—I think that's who—was what you might call an order for the assassination. Actually, more like permission ...'

Guerin could stand it no longer, he had to stop her. 'You really expect me to believe this, because nobody else will, file or no file.'

'They will if they see it, Stephen.' She said it so simply and convincingly, Guerin felt the room begin to fall away from him. Julia went on in the same, almost indolent, tone: 'Another one of the papers, I remember, was several pages of analysis of the political situation in the United States and the possible effect the elimination of Kennedy would have. Also around the world. I'm not a political person so I didn't pay that close attention to some of it.'

Guerin shook his head once as if to clear it, then kept it moving in sheer disbelief. 'There's never been one single piece of evidence that points to the Reds. Nothing ... not one thing.'

Somewhere in the file they said that—I mean, that it shouldn't even be carried out unless they could get someone else to do it for them, someone with completely different politics or a psychopath, or some kind of deception, anyway.'

'Was Oswald mentioned, or anyone else you've heard associated with the case?'

Her attitude turned slightly patronizing. 'They used cover names, Stephen—what kind of idiots do you think they have in Havana? Besides, I've been in Cuba myself these last few years, remember? So how could I possibly have your knowledge of the different investigations and discoveries?' She was right, he was not thinking clearly. 'Look,' she went on, 'there were lots of things I probably don't remember, papers on alternative ways to do it, contingencies if it came out that the regime there was responsible —they wanted revenge for Playa Girón, I suppose, but they weren't anxious to provoke another. I will say that one of the plans someone had put forth sounded very much like the way I understand it really happened. Sniping at a car, you know, and the rest of it.'

She had to wait a long time for him to respond. Finally he got up and began to pace. 'Someone wants to turn the world upside down.'

'What business is that of yours? What they do with it, I mean. You have your assignment, and it's going to be all you can do just to bring it off.'

'Who wants it, Julia?'

'What do you mean? The American government. Why else are we here?'

He stopped pacing and looked at her. Julia met his gaze evenly, as she always did. 'Is it the "Element"?' he asked.

'How would I know?'

'You knew enough not to trust us, enough to be afraid you might be killed on the beach. I have no idea who told you, perhaps a lover, but I've come to have some respect for their opinions.'

She attacked the ashtray with her cigarette and her face lit with anger. She was naked and totally unselfconscious, her back straight and her neck arched like an angry, strutting bird; Guerin thought she was utterly, inexpressibly beautiful. 'How dare you start a political discussion at a time like this—what kind of a man are you? And then you start in again about my lovers. It's petty and beneath you, but you don't have any pride. You disgust me sometimes, Stephen.'

Guerin failed to react. His manner was simple and relentless. 'That didn't take, Julia. Is it the "Quarry Element"?'

She nodded solemnly.

16

'What good is it?' Julia wanted to know. 'How can it be worth all this?' She turned the collar of her thin spring coat up around her neck. The waves on Lake Zurich, lapping at the abutment a few feet away, were showing more chop every minute as the wind bore down from the high peaks to the north and west. Guerin signalled for the waiter and ordered Julia another cup of hot chocolate—her third. 'Why is it so important to them especially, Stephen?'

Guerin drew heavily on his cigar and glanced at the access bridge, the restaurant being settled on a small manmade island, before answering. 'Have you ever heard of the Zinoviev letter?' She shook her head. 'It's an almost unbelievable example of how a tiny piece of paper can affect a whole nation. Back in the twenties it was purported to be a letter from the Soviets to British union leaders, offering them help and encouraging revolution. Public opinion was so aroused they overturned the Labour government and put in the Tories. Later, it was proven that the letter had been forged by Czarist exiles in England ... who had been paid to do it by the Tories.' He fell silent, thoughtful, struck by something about what he had just said.

'Would it be an excuse to invade the island again?'

'It could have that ultimate effect. Probably the papers wouldn't be made public, I don't know; they could just be circulated within the government. Probably in the highest, most restricted circles. Otherwise you'd have absolute hysteria. But the "linas duras" would gain a hell of an edge, even without that.' He leaned forward and gripped her wrist where it lay upon the table. 'Listen, Julia, supposing, like the Zinoviev letter, they're a forgery, the whole thing is a fake?'

'That's ridiculous, I took them out of the file in the Ministry myself.'

'Someone had to tell you where to go and what to look for, exactly what to look for. Didn't they?'

'Yes, of course. A Yankee who came to one of our meetings at a private home in the suburbs, I think he called himself Henderson—I never saw him again—took me into the kitchen out of hearing and gave me the orders. Next time I went to my dead drop I was given the location of the cabinet, and what I needed to identify the file —I went right to it. I was scared to death, but there was nothing to it actually.'

The waiter brought her chocolate and they stopped talking until he removed himself. Guerin leaned close again. 'No American could have got into the Ministry, obviously, so there had to be another agent to stake out the assignment. Who could have taken the file as easily as you ...'

Julia looked noncommittal. 'You can't know that for certain.'

'Theoretically, anyway, there has to be at least one other agent operating in the Ministry of the Interior. If it was someone from your own component, you would have known it.'

'Of course. But then there are other groups still in Havana. Even now, when the resistance is dying out.'

'So it's not impossible then. And the Quarry people could profit enormously from it.'

She shook her head and the long black hair caught in the wind. He put up his hand to help bring it under control and ended by laying it alongside her cheek. She touched his hand with hers and smiled very close to his face. 'You're not always a political animal yourself, are you?' she said.

'I'm a little sorry I haven't been more political. How did you ever come to accept me for a lover?'

'Because you are very sensitive, and quite a good one. Lover, I mean. Oh, God, I wish this mess would be over soon. Stephen, if you found out somehow that those papers really were a giant hoax, what would you do?'

'Julia!' the handsomely accented voice called. Guerin had already started to turn his head because something about the way the man trod the gravel path between the tables had alerted him. Whether it was instinct or training, he also believed he could read a man's character from his walk, or merely the sound of it. Of course it was unnecessary where Peter Zahner was concerned; he had emblazoned his character across the covert political history of several great nations by a single act. Guerin's personal judgment was no less negative.

Peter was tall and blond and square-jawed, with the kind of agate blue eyes that the men who have them can seldom resist playing like a girl's. His teeth were polished to a high sheen. A real Nordic, but the subtle military air he worked so hard to convey was strictly bogus. Easily detestable from almost any of Guerin's references, the fact that he had once been the lover of this slim dark girl beside him threatened his objectivity to such an extent he was not even sure he could get through what was required of him professionally.

They had exchanged their greetings and were waiting on him. He stood and indicated a chair for Peter, but ignored the proffered handshake. Peter shrugged as if he had expected calculated rudeness. He sat close to Julia and continued to smile. Guerin watched them both for a moment, fascinated that a man who had cheated a girl who had loved, or at least trusted, him in such a way that he put her life in jeopardy could perform this sexual charade exactly as if nothing had happened. Peter stroked her arm, whispering something without moving his lips, and that was suddenly the end—Julia pulled away from him with studied contempt. 'You rotten son-of-a-bitch,' she murmured.

Peter laughed and gave it up. He swung around to Guerin as though the latter had just arrived. 'Would you identify yourself, please?'

'You were told on the phone I was coming. My name is Guerin.'

'No, that won't do ... an authorization of some kind.'

Now, at least, he knew definitely the man was an amateur. 'I'm carrying a bank draft. That'll be validation enough, I should think.'

'If I call the American consulate, will they verify you?'

'Of course not.' Guerin was starting to enjoy himself.

'Stop being so childish, Peter,' Julia said to him. 'You can reason it out without playing spy.'

He flushed a little but covered quickly. 'You don't understand, my darling. I am dealing with more than one agency.'

'You would be, of course.'

He turned condescending. 'Now would it not be stupid of me, having taken such chances and come this far, not to exploit the situation to the limit. It's only good economics, and politics too.' Summoning the waiter he ordered a Negroni.

'It might also get you killed.'

He gave Guerin what was certainly a pointed look. 'I am counting on the well-reasoned pragmatism of your friends ... and their enemies. No doubt I've irritated a great many people, besides yourself Julia, but my impression has always been that his sort'—he indicated Guerin as though he were on a platter—'cannot allow themselves the simple little emotions the rest of us cultivate in order to get through life all in a piece. You are reasonable, aren't you?' he asked Guerin.

'And regretting it more every minute.'

'If they hurt me, Julia, then they do not get the papers. If they try to trick me, then that sort of thing gets around and others, defectors and people of that sort, will not trust them.'

'Common blackmailers,' Guerin pointed out to him, 'men without politics or professional credentials, are considered to be outside the game and treated like criminals.'

'Please don't waste our time by trying to frighten me. You people cannot afford revenge. If you ever started to indulge yourselves, the bloodbath would exceed the Great Plague and World War II together.'

Guerin looked around. The early winter wind down from the near Alps had come close to emptying the garden. An old couple holding hands got up when the tree closest them bent low over the table and littered it with dry leaves. Another old man with a beard clung stolidly to his copy of the *Neue Zuricher Zeitung*. A teenage boy and girl in matching ski sweaters studied their lessons side by side, oblivious. There was no tag in sight, although of course they could be watched from anywhere along the shore, any one of a dozen buildings over there could harbour a man with binoculars, or an assassin, if they had come to that point.

'What's the matter?' Peter asked him, his voice again betraying his anxiety.

'You'd better get used to looking over your shoulder,' Guerin told him, 'you're going to be doing a lot of it. Are the Swiss police covering you?'

'Only if I snap my fingers.'

'He wouldn't dare call in the police,' Julia said.

'Oh, yes, he would.' He addressed Peter. 'I would imagine you must have some friends in the police, a man in your position?'

'In an emergency. They really don't like foreign agents here, you know. And they are very good, very efficient.'

'I'll give them that.'

'That was, of course, the unfortunate reason I was forced to ask you to come all the way over here to bargain. A man is so much safer in his own country, among friends.'

Guerin drew the bank draft from his pocket but masked it with his hands from the view of anyone looking on. 'Whatever you may have heard about the Yankee propensity to bargain doesn't hold true here. But I'm authorized to offer you a quarter of a million dollars. That's strictly take it or leave it.'

Julia muttered appreciatively: 'Sweet Jesus!'

'If you refuse and try to string it out, I go away and our people pursue other means, whatever they might be.'

'What would they be?' Peter asked.

Guerin was being quite sincere when he said: 'I don't know. I don't make decisions at that level. Two hundred and fifty thousand dollars is the sum.'

Peter was getting his confidence back, or at least a loan on it, and turned cocky very quickly. The sound of big money had had its usual aphrodisiac effect. The Swiss, and Guerin had to admit he was very American in the way he reacted to the promise of wealth, rekindled his blond Storm Trooper smile and shot it out at Julia, who was by now staring hard into the muddy residue of her cup. 'Can you imagine what we could have done with that much money if we had had it when we were together, darling? Yes, even in Cuba. And now ... perhaps you will find it in your heart to forgive me.'

Guerin felt sorry for the girl and broke in peremptorily. 'I'm a little tired of all this, Zahner. Is it a deal or isn't it?'

Peter batted his eyes in a way that was intended to show he bore his accuser no resentment and was only saddened by the other's insensitivity. 'I explained to you, Mr Guerin, that I am negotiating with your competition. It is not altogether impossible that they will offer even more. I mean the Russians. I have not contacted the Chinese, although I may yet.'

'I wouldn't,' Guerin told him listlessly, 'they refuse to play these silly little games with the rest of us—something about revolutionary morality—and they're pretty much indifferent to the goodwill of any nation ... even Switzerland. They'll just kill you if they want to.'

'You don't like Switzerland very much, do you?'

'It's businesslike,' Guerin said. 'And neutral—it affects me that way, very neutral.'

'By that you mean smug, narrow, insular ...'

'I'm going for some cigarettes,' Julia announced, standing and moving away with the same emotional thrust.

'Wait a minute, I have some ...' Peter called after her. He looked disappointed. Guerin knew better than to try to bring her back. He felt reasonably sure she would not go so far away as to put herself in jeopardy. 'Well,' said Peter, spreading his hands on the table in a gesture of acceptance, 'there is something—I don't know in what language—about a woman scorned.'

Guerin felt a strong desire to topple the man, who was much larger than himself, from his chair and kick him senseless, or dead, before he could recover. He could have carried it off had he been willing to accept the consequences, of that he was reasonably sure. The fantasy helped, however. 'I want some proof that you have the papers.'

Surprisingly, Peter reached into his pocket without hesitation and withdrew a folded piece of paper. 'I anticipated that,' he said, 'and brought one along. A lesser one, I think, having to do with contingencies, but it should be proof enough.' Guerin took it. 'There were five more sets in the file,' Peter added, 'but then I suppose you know that.'

Guerin began a systematic study of the document, not only its contents but even of the paper itself. In preparation for the original mission, he had, with customary thoroughness, researched the clerical and documentary practices of the Havana government.

The other man watched him curiously. 'Actually, I share your negative feelings about my own country,' he rambled. 'I have no doubt you think I am the worst kind of son-of-a-bitch, you have made that quite clear, but I wonder if you know what life is like in this stifling, wretched little country. Unless one is a banker it is hopeless, absolutely hopeless. I dress well, it is true, but then a man must have something to be proud of. Actually, I have a small apartment when I am in the country, not a block away from my mother and the dismal little place where I was born. But I estimate that I could work a hundred and fifty or sixty years in the foreign service without accumulating the money you offer me ... What are you doing?'

Guerin held the paper up to the light, he ran his fingers across it delicately, lingering over the type. The typewriter was probably East German, most likely a Groma; two vertical spaces were roughly equivalent to a space and a half on an American or Italian machine. It had an accent mark, that ruled out an American in any case. The grain and consistency of the paper inclined him to believe it might be Czech, and he knew the Cubans imported paper from Czechoslovakia. The form, the phrasing, everything combined to suggest that it was no forgery. Guerin found himself wishing otherwise. He did not feel any obligation to explain himself to Zahner, who in any event could not know of his real concerns—the fact that the Swiss had the file in his possession had never been seriously in doubt.

Guerin glanced at his watch. 'I'll wait twenty-four hours for a decision from you. But that's it. Is this place all right?'

'I suppose so,' Zahner said with an air of indifference. Guerin laid down some money for the cheque and stood. 'Wait a minute, you are in such a hurry,' Zahner complained, digging through the pockets of his tight Italian suit for something. Finally he handed Guerin a business card. 'This is a friend of mine at the Grossdammer Bank. Please stop by and show him your draft and discuss the matter with him. He will, in turn, report to me.' For some reason he included the information, 'I went to school with him.'

'What did you study?' asked Guerin, as he walked away.

Ahead of him he could see Julia; she had left the island and was standing in the waterfront park staring out across the turbulent green water. She looked child-like and quite desolate. Nevertheless, when he caught her up and took her along with him, he could not prevent himself from saying, 'I can't forgive you for that bastard,' in a voice tight with anguish. If he had expected one of her declarations of self-sufficiency in retort, he was disappointed; Julia came away from the scene in silence.

17

They went back to their hotel along a twisting pedestrian walkway that ran behind the buildings that lined the river. On the opposite shore were more of the same ornate ancient structures, lighted in muted colours from below. The slashing green water hurtling down from the mountains passed close by them to the lake. Guerin had been along it many times before and always loved it, should have at least admired it now in this penumbral fall twilight, but instead felt oppressed by it, as gloomy as the joyless heart of old Calvin, whose city this really was. Once or twice he made contact with Julia's arm in the course of helping her up or down some steps, but they had yet to speak since leaving the restaurant.

As they approached the hotel he glanced sideways and thought in the passing lights he detected tears glistening in the corner of her eye. If that was what it was, he told himself, it was astounding in a girl as self-controlled as this, and he hoped it might be related to him. He wished he could summon the right words to resolve it between them, but the spectral army of doubts and qualifications he took with him everywhere, except to work, rushed in to stifle the intent.

There was a message waiting for him at the desk requesting that he call a local number. They went up to their separate rooms, which was just as well because he had no idea who he was calling and preferred to place it in private. The voice at the other end was female and Slavic-accented, although she had answered in German. Guerin quickly switched to French in announcing himself. The girl went away and came back with a man who knew, obviously, to whom he was speaking, for he opened with a cheery, 'Hello, Kozhevnikov here,' in English.

Guerin felt like being laconic. 'You called me.'

'Ah, yes,' the Russian said, as if just remembering, 'Mr Guerin. Allow me, I am Alexander Kozhevnikov.'

'Are you sure, Mr Kozhevnikov, you have the right party, because I have no idea who you are?' Actually, Guerin was running the voice, the name, the personal characteristics through his computer. He was quite certain they had never met before, although he had known a number of Russians when he was on the Vienna station. The voice was that of a heavily-built man on the youngish side of middle-age. It seemed outwardly good-natured.

'Oh, yes, you are the one, Mr Guerin. The very one. But now you must forgive me. I speak frankly now. Very openly—we think always it is best in situations like this.'

Guerin knew that any time someone told you they were going to speak openly and frankly you were in for a bad time. 'Go on,' he urged.

'Well, yes. You see, I am in the same business as you. Only I come from over on the other side, of course. Am I clear?'

'You are frank and open.'

'Good. Now, I want to discuss with you a matter of mutual interest. I am not concerned that your telephone might be interdicted—are you?' Guerin indicated that he was not particularly. Kozhevnikov seemed buoyed by that, and became even more Rotarian in his appeal. 'Splendid! You will see, we shall negotiate this problem easily and with maximum dispatch. I refer, of course, to the matter of papers taken away from Cuba, and this man, Zahner, who is ransoming you.'

'I'm afraid I have no idea what you are talking about.'

Kozhevnikov corrected himself, as if the problem was grammatical. 'That is, blackmailing you. And us, also, as you can imagine.'

'I don't know any Zahner, Mr Kozhevnikov. I'm sorry.'

The Russian laughed tolerantly. 'Oh, you do, of course. You have just returned from him ... Mr Scofield.'

'Scofield' was an identity Guerin had used in other places a couple of years before, and it was Kozhevnikov's not very subtle way of reminding him of his vulnerability. There was enough of the provincial braggart about it to make it inoffensive, it was typically Russian, but on the other hand, however realistic you were about the sanctity of a long-range cover, it was always disturbing to have the Hostiles match two distinctly different identities; that was often very bad news indeed. He thought perhaps he would not mention it when he got home.

'I have no radical suggestions to compromise you, believe me,' Kozhevnikov said. 'What I have in mind is merely some few minutes investment to see if we cannot clarify the mutual problem which has arisen with this man.'

Guerin agreed. There was no reason not to. Kozhevnikov named a dark corner of the city and recommended an immediate rendez-vous. Guerin countered with the busiest corner of the Bahnhofstrasse in the centre of the city, not because he saw anything sinister in the Russian's choice— he knew that was simply their procedure, their style, and they followed it in drops and assignations all over the world, always under bridges or in abandoned places—but because it would be well, in case his own people had him under surveillance, to be conventional.

He hung up and went next door to Julia's room. She was sitting and staring at a grotesque picture of an alpine scene with her back to the door, smoking. The door was unlocked and he took the time to scold her for that, which she enjoyed without acknowledging it to him. When he told her he had to go out, her attitude changed and she turned around with eyes widened by curiosity. 'Who are you meeting?' she wanted to know, but he refused to tell her. There was no need to. He exacted a promise that she would not go out, would not admit anyone but him. A promise she broke within the hour.

Kozhevnikov, true to his word, had no great revelations to impart, or even a definitive plan to suggest. They strolled the large and busy avenue with the rest of the dinner crowd, pausing periodically to stare into store windows at nothing.

'I hope I am not naïve, Mr Guerin, but it seems to me

both countries, yours and mine, could be greatly harmed by these papers. Therefore, this meeting with you. To explore mutual self-interest.'

'How do you mean, to both countries?' Guerin asked blandly. 'They're your allies, not ours.'

'Ah, but surely you cannot believe we would be with the Cubans in a ... a provocation like this?' He stopped to look at Guerin and spread his hands in a way that was intended to give his words added sincerity. 'The Cubans are crazy, everybody knows that. Surely your government would not think that of us.'

'I have no idea what my government thinks of anything, Mr Kozhevnikov. I'm only an agent—if you've been told I was on a policy-making level, then your informant, who knew where I was staying, what I was after and a lot of my history, chose to lie to you about that.'

Kozhevnikov thought that over seriously. Finally he smiled and suggested a café. They headed across the street with the green light. Always obey the laws of the host country. 'Well, you can report what I say and contact could be made on the appropriate level if it would seem helpful. Is it not so?'

Guerin nodded. He was thinking that Kozhevnikov was at least a colonel, most likely in the KGB, to be carrying on discussions of this sort. It remained to be seen if he was from the Department of Disinformation.

'How much money is he asking of you?' Kozhevnikov asked, as Guerin held open the door to a *kafehaus* for him.

'A little more than what he's asking of you, I imagine.'

The Russian laughed appreciatively and then shrugged, signifying that he understood they would never get anywhere pursuing this line.

Inside, it turned out to be one of those places where old men sit reading newspapers from racks on the walls. Common enough in Zurich, it was 'alkoholfrei'. Kozhevnikov was upset, he wanted a drink, but Guerin, thinking

166

of the girl alone back at the hotel, refused to go elsewhere. He had never known, true to the stereotype, an abstemious Russian, and they generally regarded him as hopelessly austere. Yet somehow he got on well with them as a rule. Kozhevnikov had pink cheeks, broad shoulders and a slightly too-large head to go with his stumpy body, but an effective grin that belied his occupation and made him almost handsome.

'Do you like him?' Kozhevnikov asked, staring down disapprovingly at his hot chocolate.

'Who?'

'This Zahner. He is a dandy. And a sneak.'

'He'll soon be a very rich dandy and sneak, whether it's dollars, Swiss francs or roubles he's spending.'

'Dollars,' Kozhevnikov said gloomily. 'He is demanding it in dollars.'

Guerin smiled. 'I don't blame you for being angry. We call that adding insult to injury in English.'

'I understand. But if neither one would deal with him ...?'

'Nothing would be settled. It would all come out somehow, perhaps in an even more dangerous context than the present situation. At some time when we are once more ... "eyeball to eyeball".'

'I remember this phrase. Look, Mr Guerin, as one man to another, as a professional to another, do you believe what is in these papers is truthful, that the Cubans had anything to do with the assassination of Kennedy? Because I do not. From the bottom of my heart, I tell you that—I do not. I have said they were crazy, but not so crazy as this. I was in Cuba once and they were reckless and unstable people, but they love life. They are the worst revolutionaries in the history of the world, but by God they love life. And this, these papers, are death. It is not a political act, to assassinate, you know, we do not believe in this. It is always the work of individualistic romantics,

167

of madmen. Men who love death ...'

He was getting emotionally involved and it set Guerin back a little, because he had never seen a Russian or any other communist agent who had let this happen to himself. He reminded Kozhevnikov that no one in informed circles in the United States had considered it to be the act of communists at the time, nor did they now, to the best of his knowledge.

'But what,' Kozhevnikov asked him, arching one eyebrow in operatic fashion, 'if they are not genuine?'

'Have you seen them?'

'No,' the Russian admitted. He seemed to sense that Guerin had, even as he said it.

'How do you know what you're getting, then?' It was petty, but Guerin could not resist a little gamesmanship. 'Are you going to give him all that money and then find he's pedalling his old laundry bills?'

Kozhevnikov stopped being the happy peasant. 'He knows that if he did we would hound him everywhere until we had revenged ourselves. It would be a matter of principle. I told him that.'

'Well, don't worry, he has something—I saw one of the papers and it went a long way towards substantiating the rest. I'm only sorry to say that everything I saw looked authentic as hell ... paper, type, style and content.'

Kozhevnikov looked sober. 'Also unfortunately, everything I know of you would incline me to trust your judgment in such matters. Still, I must say that we have our most serious doubts. I wish I could tell you the foundations for these reservations. I wish that was possible ...' He shook his head.

'Is that why you asked for this meeting, to tell me they wouldn't be worth bargaining for, since you knew they were fakes?'

'No, no, no, I cannot accept that. You know I would not insult you in such a way.' He leaned across the table, dipped and withdrew his sleeve from the residue of his hot chocolate, but then again proceeded with more intensity of emotion than Guerin was accustomed to. 'Listen, Mr Guerin, let me speak frankly and openly, there is grave concern on our part for these papers. And their implications. I am in contact with you only because you are the man here and now, negotiating. You can be certain that contacts are being made in other quarters and at other levels. If only we could work together . . .'

'Why don't you just out-bid us?'

Kozhevnikov actually groaned. An old man sitting at an adjoining table looked around his newspaper at them. 'If only it was so simple. You know it is not. All that we are asking of you is to co-operate in the same manner that we did after the assassination itself. Your people asked us for data, for all our files on Oswald and much more to verify your commission. We did so, we worked together, if not like brothers then at least like two great peoples with mutual problems and interests.'

'Very impressive. I'm certainly sympathetic, Mr Kozhevnikov. But what is it that you are *not* saying? Why don't you simply advise the proper levels of the United States government about your concerns? I'll do you the credit of suggesting that you know it's absolutely absurd to approach me in this way. I'm impressed that you know all about me, but if you do, then why are you wasting your time? And mine?'

Kozhevnikov thought that over for a minute. 'You see, it is precisely because we know all about you, Mr Guerin, that we do approach. We know so much, we know you are not one of those people in your organization which seek to provoke and create desperate relations between our two countries. That is why you should help us. We know everything.' He sat back with the look of a man who has made his point to his own satisfaction.

'You bastards,' Guerin said with some feeling, 'you've got half our agents on your payroll.'

The Russian smiled. 'You remember when Nikita Sergei-vich told that to your Eisenhower, and he did not believe him? But seriously, I would urge you to co-operate—not betray—for this very reason. Your system has gone quite mad. We understand, we have experienced similar but not quite so decadent a sickness under the late ... You know who I mean. The ogre. Of course we survived, because the country, the ideology, was healthy. I honestly wish you to survive too. Many of us feel that—again, out of self-interest. Yours is a great and powerful nation, so no one hopes it will go berserk on this small planet.'

Guerin felt such distress, such pain, he could not remain where he was; he stood up without warning, almost knock-ing over his chair. 'Goddammit, quit patronizing me. We'll settle our problems ourselves and you keep your bloody hands out of it.'

Kozhevnikov was surprised and alarmed at the reaction he had elicited. Also, he constitutionally did not like the attention they were attracting. Without the slightest self-consciousness, he reverted to a heavy-handed authori-tarianism and snapped out: 'Sit down and be quiet! People are watching.'

Guerin was beyond caring. His cover was fully blown for everyone who counted, anyway. He leaned on the edge of the table and lowered his voice to a near-whisper, not to avoid scrutiny but rather to drive home the words with sibilant fervency. 'This whole thing is a phoney and we both know it. You asked me here to double me. You're scared stiff of what's in those papers and you'd give any-thing if I'd just hand the whole deal over along with my career and my soul. You were counting on my disillusion-ment with the mess we're in. But you missed something when you researched me—if I get tired of being lied to and used by opportunists or fascists, I'm not going to look to you to change it. I'm not a defector, I just don't have that mentality.'

Kozhevnikov sighed. He was no longer concerned about the old men around them, either. 'It is true that I would recruit you, if that was possible. But never mind, the situation, the potential for great disaster in your organization is not, as you say, "phoney". That, and the danger in these damned papers, is real. And very grave. Is it not, Mr Guerin?'

'I know,' Guerin admitted. He felt his face; it was warm. His ears rang. There was nothing more to say, so he turned and left the restaurant.

It was not quite cold enough to freeze down here in the valley and a fine rain had begun to fall. Guerin pulled the collar of his English raincoat up around his neck. The mountains were blotted out by low-lurking clouds, though some small lights flickered through the misty rain from nearby hills. The streets, save for occasional cars, were now nearly empty. A young couple under a leaky umbrella passed him, laughing, wet, hurrying to somewhere sane, and totally indifferent to him, who perhaps, in some small way, held responsibility for their very lives. In the far distance he could perceive a small, brightly lit lake steamer as it surged out across the black water and into the mist, as if off the edge of the world. He could have looked for a cab but he needed the rain.

18

He was only a block from the hotel when he became aware of the Citroen. It came towards him slowly, huddling against the kerb like a limping roach with its lights pointed directly into his eyes. A cold hand squeezed his heart and he looked around. Ahead of him was the darkened doorway of a pension that could provide cover if they intended to come up over the kerb for him. But if it was locked, not unusual in Zurich even at this early hour, then it would merely frame him for a gunman or trap him for a kidnapping. That was all there was, however, and he would have to time it just right to reach the door at the same time the car pulled alongside, and yet not give anything away. He was frightened, but at the same time a little pleased that he could still think coolly and rationally.

He had a moment to regret his behaviour with Kozhevnikov, hating the thought that what might be his last professional confrontation, excluding dying, had been one full of naïvety and self-pity on his part. He also had long enough to tell himself that was a ridiculous concern. The man next to the driver leaned out of the car and Guerin tensed in preparation for a hard, swift glide to the pavement; he was certain they were going to kill him, and only wished he knew why.

The man called out something to him. He stayed primed, not answering, while the car closed to within a few yards. The man called again and this time he heard his name. But he reflected unhappily that it seemed to be common knowledge among the intelligence services of the Western World and beyond. There was nothing else to do now but take his chances. They pulled alongside and could kill him easily if they wished. He simply stared the man in the face—young with white hair and white brows and almost translucent eyes, a near-albino from what Guerin could see in the dark. Oddly distinctive for an agent under any circumstances.

'Climb Mount Eiger,' the man said softly.

'The Jungfrau is better,' Guerin replied, slopping up the rigid formality of the countersign, which correctly contained eight words, out of irritation and fatigue.

Apparently they did not care, because they accepted it without comment. The white-haired man reached behind him to open the door. Guerin stepped in quickly and demanded their papers.

The driver introduced himself as Lombardi as he handed his wallet back over his right shoulder. Guerin checked them meticulously; they seemed legitimate, the almost infinitesimal 'mistakes' put there to foil potential forgers were in their proper place. He returned them and waited but the other man made no attempt to prove himself and it was necessary to repeat the request. 'He doesn't carry them,' Lombardi explained, and Guerin asked why not, although he thought he knew.

The white-haired man confirmed: 'I'm on Staff D—the name is Martin.'

At least, Guerin consoled himself, there would be none of the ambiguity he had faced with Homer; this one was clearly an assassin, or an 'executive', to call him by one of the more self-conscious euphemisms in a professional lexicon which was surfeited with them. But all the more strange that Martin was so unusual looking; perhaps he simply coloured his features any way he wished before carrying out an assignment. Maybe that was an advantage. The qualities required of an efficient 'executive' were so special they might be expected to supersede more ordinary requirements, he supposed. Looking at the indifferent back of Martin's head he suffered one of those painful literary-isms when the phrase 'the whiteness of the whale' passed through his mind. Turning the 'executive's' pigmentation into a symbol of evil by exercising Melville was scarcely defensible for a man who had made his life decisions. Guerin, not unlike many of his fellows, felt uneasy in the presence of Staff D, and he put the blame for his morbidity on that. He noticed Martin wheezing slightly and inquired about it, presumably out of politeness but really because he wanted to hear the man talk.

'Rain bothers me.' Martin tapped his chest. 'Black lungs.'

Guerin thought it was something more prosaic, like asthma. They picked up speed and began to cruise about the city. He waited for them to move.

After a while Lombardi asked him how the assignment was going. He filled in the background, omitting for the moment his encounter with the Russian, and told them he expected a definitive answer one way or the other by the next day.

'Do you think he'll sell to us?' Lombardi wanted to know.

'I think there's a good chance.'

'Why do you say that?'

'That's just my evaluation of the man. He's scared. He's running. We're the ones he stole them from in the first place. We would be the more highly motivated to punish him if it doesn't come through.'

'How did you know he was so frightened?' Lombardi pressed.

Guerin settled back on the seat. It was obvious they were going to be at him for a while. The white head of the 'executive' remained erect and straight ahead, no questions from him. 'He was nice to me,' Guerin explained, and his interlocutor laughed.

Lombardi pointed out that Zahner might sell to the Russians if they offered him asylum in addition.

'He wouldn't be happy over there. That's not his style.'

'What is his style?' Lombardi asked.

'I wasn't implying anything subtle by that,' Guerin told him. 'He looks like a ski instructor and has the soul of an ambitious shopkeeper. The only thing that's got him this far is a certain amount of cunning, which he thinks is intelligence.'

'Very literary. Maybe when you retire you can write one of those exposés of the Firm.' He said it good-naturedly enough, but Guerin wondered just what the hell he meant by that.

174

'And the girl,' Martin put in.

Guerin said he did not understand.

'The Fernandez girl is what got him this far.' He turned and smiled at Guerin.

Oddly, even with the blank, albino-like eyes, his smile was not sinister. Guerin thought to himself that there was no God-given guarantee that a man's character had to show in his face. It would not do to believe that, anyway. 'The girl made a mistake, but there's no evidence that she intended things to go this way. They didn't think so at the House, anyway, or they wouldn't have sent her out.'

Martin smiled again, less pleasantly this time, and then turned back to stare through the rain-stricken windshield. Guerin wondered if he had protested a bit too much. The only sounds for a few moments were the hiss of the tyres on the wet pavement and the flapping of the wiper blades. The rain had built up and now the streets were completely deserted. But then, Zurich was a nine o'clock town in good weather.

'Why did you meet the Russian?' Lombardi asked.

Guerin was not surprised that they knew. He had had that familiar feeling that people were all around him, watching, since the moment he had set foot on Swiss soil, some 'friendly', some Hostile, and not a lot to choose between them for practical purposes. 'He asked me to. He called me where I was staying.'

'How did he know?'

'They seem to have the whole deal pretty well under glass.'

'Yes,' Lombardi agreed, 'they've been on you since you landed in Berne. Of course that doesn't explain anything.'

'The girl,' stated the white-haired man.

Guerin made no comment. He hoped Lombardi would. But instead he asked, 'What did Kozhevnikov want?'

Guerin measured his own words. There was a good possibility that they knew that, too. Kozhevnikov might even be working for the Firm. But which faction? God, he thought to himself, anything is possible now. 'He started by saying that the papers in Zahner's possession might be inimical to the best interests of both our countries and that we ought to consider co-ordinating the whole business, or at least consulting.'

Lombardi seemed concerned. 'That's extraordinary. Don't you think so?'

Guerin was beginning to suspect that they did not know what was in the papers, and he felt like rubbing their noses in it. 'That judgment depends on the contents of the file itself and how you interpret its ramifications.' Silence from the front seat. 'Do you have any instructions for me? Where are you going?' They had been driving out along the lake but now the car was turned around towards the city again.

'Back to your hotel,' Lombardi answered. Guerin believed him and breathed a little easier. 'Nothing complicated about your orders. Do everything you possibly can to settle it quietly with this bastard tomorrow, but if he doesn't come across you call this number immediately.' He handed back a plain card bearing a single phone listing. 'You don't have to identify yourself, simply say "credit denied". After that it's no longer any concern of yours, understand? He took his eyes off the road long enough to look back at Guerin.

'I thought getting ahold of these papers was top priority. That's the way they told it back at the House.'

'If you can't buy them tomorrow it's no longer any concern of yours,' Lombardi repeated like a patient school-master.

Guerin resented it, although he knew he had no right to and it would not do him any good. 'You're certain you have the authorization for this?' He had managed to make it more of an assertion than a question.

'It's our ass if we don't, isn't it?' Lombardi said. Martin

bobbed his head slightly in agreement.

'Not necessarily,' Guerin replied. He was beginning to feel as gloomy about the prospects of winning as losing.

'There's one more thing,' Martin said, pausing either for dramatic effect or to light a cigarette. Obviously this was going to be within his special province, because it was the first instruction he had offered. 'After you call us, you watch for this car. When it arrives, you send the girl down with her bag and everything. Tell her it's orders, tell her you're going back separately, anything you want along that line that sounds plausible. Then wait at least a quarter of an hour and return to the embassy in Berne for trans-shipment as before. Simple?'

Guerin's palms had begun to dampen. Jesus, he thought to himself, where do they get these guys—recruit them from the Mafia, the Klan, the Ustashi? Too young for an SS alumnus. Jesus! 'Why?' he demanded.

Lombardi looked back at him again without saying anything. Guerin leaned forward on the seat and repeated his question.

'Just do it that way,' Martin said sharply.

And Lombardi singsonged: 'Ours not to reason why . . .'

'Look, this girl was given the whole laundry when we were in DC. I was there for most of it. There was no proof of treason or defection or anything except making a damned stupid move out of fear. They wouldn't have let her come over here with me otherwise. She's trying to make up for it.'

'What the fuck has all that got to do with anything?' Lombardi grumbled.

'I'm trying to tell you there must be some mistake. Who-ever told you to take the girl screwed-up somewhere.' He knew his anxiety was naked but there was no way of hiding it.

'No mistake,' Martin said, 'she goes with me.'

'The hell you say. I'm taking her back where she can

at least get some kind of hearing. The girl's innocent, a goddamned amateur who panicked, it's not like she was one of us ...'

'A what?' Lombardi's voice went up in surprise that sounded genuine. He exchanged glances with Martin. Guerin felt his stomach falling; he guessed what was coming. 'She's an amateur, huh? She's been with the Firm longer than you have.'

'Matter-of-fact, she's got a little too professional,' Martin threw in. He seemed to feel it ought to be amusing, because he forced a laugh with it.

Guerin countered, but without conviction. 'She was recruited in Cuba when the government executed her fiancé. She's been there six years.'

'Two years,' Lombardi said. 'She was put in by plane two years ago with a dead relative's cover. Within six months she was in the Ministry of the Interior. She's good. No denying it.'

'Too good,' the 'executive' reiterated.

'But I saw her file.'

'That means a lot these days,' Lombardi said contemptuously.

'Anybody can put anything into a file,' his partner added. 'And everybody has their own files, anyway.'

Guerin sank back against the cold upholstery. The rain was beginning to slacken but the streets would be empty now until dawn. He wondered if Julia was worried about him; he had been gone a long time. When they turned into the street leading to his hotel, he agreed to give the girl up. The two men in the front seat did not make anything of his acquiescence, but accepted it as stating the obvious. The air whistled softly through Martin's lungs.

The car glided to a spongy stop in front of the hotel, and they parted without another word. Guerin did not go in immediately, but stood looking down the street where the car had gone. He pulled his coat collar up against

the falling mist. A man with no identification, no papers—
did he even carry a social security card?—was something
terrifying. If one was prepared to become an institutiona-
lized killer the whole power of a modern nation-state was
evidently marshalled to guarantee him freedom from the
regimen of cards, numbers and files that bound the rest
of us from birth to death.

Down at the end of the block, one of those endless,
faceless little men, wearing an outsized raincoat, was
watching him from the shelter of a doorway. Guerin turned
his back on him—what did it matter?

19

Peter Zahner was first to speak as Guerin came into the
room, but it was limited to a sullen, 'Hello'. Julia had
opened the door and stood back silently, watching the
two men. He was careful to lock the door behind him, and
now that the death-seeker was in the room with them he
went so far as to draw the blind and lower the lights. Julia
knew that he detested histrionics, and was surprised, but
he also hated the idea of dying by mistake, as a result of
someone's substandard marksmanship. Assassins, in life
as opposed to art, where generally clumsy, stunted people.

'What the hell are you doing here?' Guerin asked him,
with some fatigue but no particular rancour. He took a
chair in the corner which gave him a view of the door
and was sufficiently removed from the window. Julia was
on the bed between them. He turned to her. 'Why did
you let him in?'

'Look at him,' she said.

The rosy cheeks were gone, turned drawn and grey, and
his eyes seemed almost glazed. The man had grown up in

an afternoon. Guerin watched him trying to light a cigarette and felt something akin to sympathy.

'I want to sell you the papers, please. Now.'

'Do you have them with you?'

'No. I wanted to ... to bring them ... only to get this over with quickly, but I was afraid. They could be watching you, as they were me.' The cigarette quivered between his lips. He tried to force a smile and produced a grotesque.

Pity, pity, Guerin thought, try to pity him. He is a large beautiful man who wears clothes well and has the misfortune to be a petty-minded coward. A coward without sensibility; but then, he reminded himself, one could still pity the unforgivable. Someone had tried to kill him, that was obvious, and they would no doubt succeed ultimately, that too was obvious. A lesson there for himself; once they determined to kill you, once it had become an imperative of the profession, there was nowhere to go, no one to turn to. That was true on either side. A canon to be shared with organized crime.

Guerin asked him, 'Who tried to kill you?' and the man started, as if that was the most amazing insight.

'I ... have run away from the hospital. They could not keep me there once I had decided I had to get rid of those papers in order to survive. No doctor could make me as safe as you can. Please ...'

'I asked who tried to kill you?'

'A Latin man, I think a Cuban.' He coughed violently and had to struggle to regain his breath. 'The communists!'

Guerin did not think so, or at least had his doubts, but he kept them to himself a while longer. 'How?'

'I had the file with me. You see, I had mailed it out to myself for protection.' He paused, as sick as he was, and looked to Guerin for approval for an obvious gambit he had learned from the movies. He had to go on without it. 'I could have mailed it out again, but I was afraid it would not come back in time for tomorrow. If by then you had made the best price. I'm not a fool, I know you people can be as violent as the others.'

Guerin was afraid he would talk himself up over the threshold of his courage; he did not want that, and urged him to get on with it.

'I didn't know what to do with it, so I took it to a friend. I had it sealed, and this man, I knew, was a real Swiss; he would never open it. He lives right here in Zurich, I grew up with him, and this, as you no doubt know, is one of the most law-abiding cities in the world ...'

'Come on, what happened?' Guerin looked at Julia, hoping he might read some of the same irritation he felt in her face. But it was not there, and he had to remind himself that now he knew she was a trained agent, a professional like himself, in order to lessen the disappointment.

Zahner was beginning to feel so sorry for himself, or at least was so sick at the recollection of what had happened to him, there seemed to be some danger that he might cry. Even Guerin hoped that would not happen. Julia, her glance told him, also hoped.

'Anyway, on the stairs going to my friend's place, a Cuban, I am now almost certain that was what he was, came up behind me. He must have been following. Something about his footsteps, some instinct—I have been in the diplomatic service seventeen years now ... At any rate, I was alerted. He called my name from behind but I turned only in part, while I kept on moving ahead, upwards. That was the thing that saved my life. In his hand, partly hidden under a newspaper, he has a device. Whatever it is, it makes a crackling sound and out comes these ... fumes. But he was too far away, beneath me by several steps, and I had not really turned to him the way he wants. There is an odour, not unpleasant, but ... it makes me ill very quickly. I started vomiting, but I held on to the file with a death grip. Almost a real death grip.' He permitted himself a smile, as if, having gone through a catharsis, he could better face the horror now than a few moments before. Guerin knew what that felt like.

'Why didn't he keep after you?'

The blond man hesitated. 'I suppose the way I yell. Everyone hears me and came running.'

Guerin understood that he meant 'screamed', but that was all right; everyone was entitled to scream under those circumstances.

'What did they do to him?' Julia asked Guerin.

She was still playing her part, but then there was no way yet of her knowing what he had been told. 'It was prussic acid under compression in a glass tube. Forms a gas. If he hadn't been going away from it when it was discharged, he would have died almost instantly. Looks very much like a heart attack to a civilian medic, unless the executioner is sloppy and gets close enough to leave little shards of glass in the victim's face. That's happened.' His explanation had caused Zahner to lose whatever colour he had regained since his arrival. 'You're lucky,' Guerin told him, 'I don't think that business has been used very often, but when it has it's never failed to be successful, to my knowledge.'

'What about him, the assassin, how did he survive?' Julia wanted to know.

'He takes an antidote for three days running before the dispatch. Then he has to break an ampule of amyl nitrite in a handkerchief immediately afterwards and inhale it. It wasn't your screaming that kept him from following up, it was panic to get to that breath of life.'

'I must say, you are very clinical about it,' Zahner pouted.

Guerin smiled malevolently. He looked at Julia and thought she was smiling too. 'You can hardly expect,' he told the Swiss, 'that we should care whether you live or die. We'll take the file if you offer it, but if they kill you tomorrow I sure don't give a damn. And, I might add, they probably will.'

'Maybe I won't sell it to you, then.'

'Yes you will. It's relative, but you're still safer without them in your possession than you are with them.'

'I have put myself under the protection of the Zurich police since this afternoon. They are very good, you know —better even than the American police.'

'If you had, they would never have let you come here. Now let's transact our business—where is the file now?'

'I will have to take you.'

'I suppose it's at either the airport or the train station, isn't it? In a locker.'

Zahner looked hurt. 'How did you know? It's at the train station.'

'You haven't failed to do the obvious yet, no reason to think you'd change.'

Peter attempted a cocky grin. 'I hope fervently, Mr Guerin, that after I have given this file to you, someone kills you for it.'

The file was where Zahner had said it would be. Guerin took it into the men's room to check it over in privacy and found it intact. He brought it out and showed it to Julia, and she agreed.

'We have it,' he said to her, 'are you happy?'

'I don't think so.'

'Excited, then?'

'Yes, that ... a little.'

Zahner stood between them, sweating in the cold, two feet away but hearing nothing because these two people did not exist for him beyond his need to please them in order to be set free. His head turned from one to the other like a puppet's. 'Will you give me my money, please?'

Guerin regarded him silently for a moment, then removed the envelope from his pocket and handed it over. It had occurred to him to refuse to pay, and there was no doubt he could have got away with it, the man was so desperate, but in the end he decided to play things straight right up until the end. There was always the chance that Zahner would get back just enough of his courage to act the spoiler, to inform. Anyway, it was closer to Guerin's temperament to do it this way.

'We never did get that cheque approved by your friend in the bank, you know.'

Zahner looked as if he wished Guerin had not reminded him. 'It will have to do. I trust you. Am I free to go now?'

'Yes, God help you. But I should tell you, someone has been watching our hotel, so it's only reasonable to think they're around here somewhere right now. I'd call the police, if I were you, and tell them someone accosted you and you want an escort home.'

'They would think I was an idiot,' Zahner protested, 'and it might well go on my record at the Ministry, too. So please allow me to govern my own affairs from this moment.' He turned to Julia, flashing some of the confidence he had been handed with the cheque. 'Julia, my dear, I know how you must feel, but . . .'

Calmly, sounding rather bored, the girl cut him off again. 'You're such a contemptible bastard, Peter, why don't you just leave.'

'Very well,' he said, patting his pocket, 'but you'll never see this much money again in your lifetime.'

He turned and stalked out of the almost deserted station, his heelplates tapping out a new rhythm of success that was reflected in his stride. Julia and Guerin watched him go.

'I know,' she said, 'why I detest him, but why do you— simply because I slept with him?'

'Think that if you want.'

'You never commit yourself, do you? To other people, I mean. In a more civilized way you're almost as big a bastard as he is.'

He took her arm. 'I have to talk to you about serious things . . . if I knew where the hell to go.'

'That's what I mean.' She was furious with him for his absorption in the business at hand, when she wanted help at hating Peter.

They went out through the front doors of the station. The rain had ended but the streets shone with its residue where light leaked from the good burghers' hermetically sealed windows. Drawing in the cold sweet air, Guerin remembered times when he had thought he would have been satisfied to live in Switzerland the rest of his life. He might yet find out, he thought.

Julia cooled down to ask him if he believed Peter would get away with the money and live happily ever after? 'Maybe. Whoever told you life was fair? In fact, if he were a bit smarter or a little less arrogant I'd say he had an excellent chance.'

'Why are we going somewhere to talk—why not back to the hotel?'

He took her across the street to a little *tabac* on the corner. They went inside because this was not a time to remain in the open. The gun was with him, in his raincoat pocket, and, while he would have liked to lay it on the table, it was enough to remove the safety and keep his hand close to it. When they were settled at a table, he answered her question: 'Because I'm not going back to the hotel with you, I'm taking the file to a man in Geneva. You'll need this.' And he gave her the gun, although he knew it was wrong.

20

The train ride to Geneva was brief and painful. Guerin had chosen the draughts and wooden benches of third class because he preferred to be among people and the open construction allowed him a wider view of the comings and goings of potential enemies. Still, the pain had nothing to do with physical conditions. He was facing a decision he did not want to make, for which he lacked sufficient information, and one that had implications far beyond his own survival. His professional life had always been a succession of weighted and blurred options, many of them critical in some way, some carrying the implication of life and death for numbers of people, but never before had he felt this ambivalence, this paralysis of the will. In the past, until the recent past, he had felt the support of an entity he respected, trusted and believed in. Now even the Firm had joined the rest of the world as a potential enemy. He was irrevocably alone.

Sitting in the citreous night lights of the railroad car, lulled by the clacking of the rails, he stared out at the scenery he could not see but remembered well from previous visits. An old peasant woman opposite gnawed on an endless piece of garlic sausage. Occasionally the retreating storm allowed the moon to burst through upon the snow that covered the landscape around the train at the higher altitudes. As a student, Guerin had come this way on much the same sort of night, travelling with a girl from the upper classes, which he had hoped to seduce both collectively and individually. They were on their way to Geneva to meet her parents but instead left the train at some station chosen at random simply because they felt an overwhelming desire to get out and romp around in that pristine blue fantasy world beyond the windows. He remembered it, but didn't believe it.

It was necessary to wait several hours before going to the University and he spent them wandering the rag-tag pre-dawn streets in the neighbourhood where Rousseau was born. He had been a long time without sleep, nor was any in sight, but he was grateful for the additional time to think things through. He regretted not having confronted Julia with what he knew about her; it would be easier all around if he could be certain of what might happen to her as a result of what he was considering doing.

Breakfast in a student café near the University buoyed him considerably, particularly the entire pot of thick black French coffee he consumed, which attacked both his stomach and his fatigue with equal ferocity. He watched the kids gathering in the cafés and in bunches along the street with their arms full of books, muffled against the early chill sharpened by the night's rain, their faces flushed, eyes full of languor, mockery, gaiety; talking gossip and arguing philosophy even at that hour. There was so much regret in that sight, nostalgia for his own innocence and the tragedy of being removed from his children, but also there was some of a continuing mixed-melancholy that was not without satisfaction. For after all, most of these young ones, however much they were supposed to represent hope for the future, would realistically never reach a point where they would be condemned, or allowed, to make the hard decisions that affect man's fate. In that he was presumably luckier than them.

The whole ploy with Dr Fortin was the result of sheer coincidence. The professor had done odd jobs for the Firm before, and Guerin had happened to be the courier-contact on two or three occasions when he was on the Vienna station.

'I must have it today,' he told Fortin, when he finally caught him coming out of his 8.00 a.m. seminar on Educational Linguistics. He had not specifically told him that he was applying for his services on behalf of the Firm, and therefore he would be paid according to the usual fee schedule, but the professor naturally inferred it. Guerin was relieved that he did.

Fortin agreed reluctantly. He would have to turn over another seminar to a graduate assistant, but, if he worked through lunch and the computers were available, it was possible he could have something later in the afternoon, depending of course on what the materials were. Guerin showed him the first page but asked that he not examine the rest carefully until he was absolutely alone.

'These are in Spanish,' Fortin said, frowning.

'All of them. Do you have examples from Guevara, Roa and other principals in the government in 1963?'

'I think so, I'll go through the files. I'll need a good-sized piece of one of them, though.'

'There's a two and a half page evaluation by Guevara.'

'Good. He was prolific, so we have quite a bit on him. The problem is the Spanish. You've never brought me anything in this language, and I'm afraid we've worked very little with it here.'

'The fact is, these papers are a hundred times more important than anything you've ever worked on.'

Fortin, a relentlessly Gaulic type anyway with his short stocky build and Breton head characterized by its squareness, thick hair and heavy brows and eyes that seemed to be perpetually squinting out to sea, arched one of those brows and asked, 'You are, of course, including Aeschulus, Tetrarch and the Dead Sea Scrolls.'

'If you have any kind of political sensibility at all, Doctor, I think you'll agree with me after you've read them. I can only beg you to give me the most accurate estimate possible.'

He could see the lights fading-up behind those shrewd fisherman's eyes, and knew the man had just shifted gears from pedant to scientist, from profit to inquiry. Guerin was satisfied; he would need all the commitment he could get.

'May I bring Solange, Miss Dubussche, into consultation on this?'

'Absolutely not. I must have your word of honour that

you will never reveal the contents of these papers to anyone. It's that important.'

Fortin assented. Now he was impatient to get at them.

Guerin asked if there was anywhere at the University that he might be allowed to sleep, and Fortin sent him to the faculty club with a note asking that he be extended all privileges. It would certainly be honoured, Guerin mused, because so many of the members had at one time or another received remuneration from the Firm, or MI6, or perhaps even Hostiles of various hues. It was only a microcosm of all the rest of Switzerland in that respect.

He slept fitfully, ate a few bites of lunch in the faculty dining room and wandered through the city again, killing time. Wandering and killing time were conduct he understood well, and he had never doubted the necessity for this or hundreds of other empty, deadening skills. But all that had been in the service of the Firm, and now the desperate self-control a man needed to pass long empty hours on the edge of an abyss was marshalled to defend the needs of his own conscience. There was a feeling of loss, of terror, and of a certain satisfaction in being a rogue agent. For he could never go back to the Firm, or more accurately would never be forgiven by it; whatever Fortin told him, the mere fact of his coming here had been a Rubicon-act. Like a man condemned to death by his doctor, he walked the streets and lakefront of Geneva and looked into the faces of others for the answer, without expecting to find one.

Every time he called Fortin he was told by the departmental secretary that the professor was occupied and could not be disturbed for any reason. Once, Guerin tried to explain that he was the reason the man had cloistered himself in the first place, that it was to serve his interests and therefore he ought logically to have access, but that argument made no headway. It was not until after six that he was able to make contact. Fortin, his voice rusty with fatigue but nevertheless excited, urged him to hurry over to the Computer Services Building. Guerin hurried for many reasons, not the least of which was the fact that Julia had been alone far too long.

'Of course I did not take as much time for the evaluation as I should have,' Fortin said in his best analytical tone. 'Many of the common words are used, no doubt of that. However, there is something self-conscious about their use. I cannot prove that mathematically, but I feel it.' He looked at Guerin with something like merriment, his eyes as bright as if he were suffering from tuberculosis or hysteria. 'Will you allow me some instincts in this matter? I confess I have used them before without telling you, and yet your people have never had occasion to regret it.'

Guerin was anxious to get on with it. He stared absently through the glass at some pretty girls in white smocks playing with the computers in an adjoining room. 'The only instincts I ever trust are those of scientists.'

'Bravo. Because I have a great many strong feelings about this material, and some serious questions, my friend, which I will get to later.'

Guerin nodded, as if to say he would pay that price gladly for the information he needed—only hurry!

'Now it's Guevara that interests us primarily. The distribution of sentence lengths is not unlike that found in his early work, the treatise on guerilla warfare, for instance ...' Guerin felt his stomach falling away—he had risked everything for nothing. 'On the other hand,' the Professor said, and it was necessary for Guerin to pull himself back for the rest of it, 'it is totally different than his later work, particularly the material he sent from Bolivia or wherever else he was during the last years of his life. A rather bad forgery, I would say, overall.' He decided to qualify that. 'Good to the eye, perhaps, but not nearly good enough to fool these.' He patted the humming computer next to him. Guerin also put out his hand and stroked the purring metallic beast.

Fortin went on, 'Everything else I could match-up tends to confirm the Guevara analysis. I've written it out for you, here ...' He handed some papers to Guerin, who did not want them, would not need them. 'There was a paragraph about the military situation in the advent of American action should the deception be discovered, supposedly by Raoul Castro, and that was unequivocally written by someone else. Perhaps they are like every other bureaucracy in the world, and it was written by some clever secretary, but I doubt it.'

'A forgery,' Guerin murmured to himself, illogically awed by the enormity of what he had, after all, suspected right along. 'All of it?' he asked.

'I should think so. In fact, although the file bears several names I would say that probably one and no more than two people were responsible for the whole of it.' He added. 'I must say, you sound relieved.'

'You know by now what the implications were.'

Fortin eyed Guerin quizzically, sat back on a stool used by the programmers and said, 'I have done my best for you, perhaps now, my friend, you would explain, within the limits of your security, a few things about this extraordinary business you have involved me in.'

Guerin glanced at his watch but the other man was not impressed. 'I'll try, but there's very little ...'

'Why did you bring this to me? Why was it not sent back to your own people, where obviously there would be less risk of its getting out?'

'We needed your expertise,' Guerin said, looking at the floor. 'We needed the best.'

'Charming. One would think you were French. But of course there must be at least a few people in the United States who could have performed this. We have published widely, particularly in connection with that work on various segments of the Bible. Besides, there are no secrets in science any more, certainly not in computer linguistics.'

'We wanted an objective opinion. Our people tend to ... ideology sometimes.'

'I don't think you are telling me the whole truth.' He raised his hands, putting a period on it.

'We seldom do.'

Fortin accepted that. He looked very grave as he said, 'Anyway, I am very happy that it isn't true.'

'So am I. So am I.'

Guerin went immediately to the railroad station and waited for a train. Now the waiting was agony; he was too agitated even to read a newspaper. What remained to be settled had to do with the girl. However much she had deceived him, he owed it to Julia, he felt, to consult her, or at least explain to her, an act which might well cost her her life. He wondered if he should have called her, but at the same time he was reasonably certain that by now the phone was tapped, and it would not serve any purpose, save for the emotional release, unless he was willing to ask her to meet him somewhere. He was not; the risk was great either way, but if he returned to the hotel room where she had holed up, at his instruction, then at least the burden of it was upon him.

21

Guerin was followed from the Zurich railroad station to his hotel, or perhaps they had been on the train with him. They might actually have been with him all the time he was in Geneva, whoever they were, if they were good. He was only thankful that no one had tried to take the file away from him. It was possible that the others were as confused and frightened as he was himself; that was usually an operative assumption, in fact. He could end it in an hour now, if only they let him alone.

He went into the hotel without checking the street, although he was more cautious inside where there were better opportunities for anyone who wanted to get in close, past the desk, which was often unmanned, and up the back stairs, avoiding the antique lift out of instinct. His head pounded wildly as he took the steps two and three at a time. A password and countersign seemed like a ridiculous luxury now. He pounded on the door and called out: 'Julia, it's Stephen!' Without answering, she threw back the bolt—for one instant his heart was in his throat; he mistook it for the priming of a certain kind of automatic—and yanked open the door. Her face, as it thrust forward at him, was gripped by a degree of emotion he never would have believed possible in her. She threw her arms around him and her voice cracked when she spoke his name. Guerin had a moment in which he almost regained his belief in the possibility of real feeling.

But then it was necessary for someone to reimpose the imperatives that would allow them to live through the next few hours; Guerin pulled himself loose, all the more roughly for his ambivalence, and closed and locked the door behind him. 'We made a hell of a good target standing there,' he said accusingly. Julia backed off and looked at him, still caught in the first flood of her relief and not quite comprehending. He saw that she was crying and had to remind himself who she was and what he had to settle with her. He ordered her to sit down quickly and listen to what was on his mind.

'I ... I'm sorry,' she stammered, 'but these last twenty hours cooped up here ... I'm afraid the strain ...' She sank back on the bed.

He smiled down at her warmly in spite of himself. 'I

don't think anyone has ever greeted me that way. I don't want to know why.'

'I guess I didn't expect to see you again. I didn't know, but I thought either they ... someone, would kill you or you'd abandon me here.'

Guerin sat down and pulled the room's one lightweight chair close in front of her. Julia felt herself pulling back involuntarily from his sudden intensity. 'I had to come back because I ... I don't know all of it, but I owe you a chance to make your move.'

'I don't understand.'

He was still clutching the briefcase which contained the file. He raised it slightly, then settled it on his lap again. 'It's a fake. The papers you risked your life to get out of Cuba are a forgery.'

She shook her head as mechanically as if she had just emerged from the water. 'I don't understand,' she repeated.

He had kept close watch on her eyes as he told her, measuring the surprise or lack of it carefully, for he would never get a better chance. 'You're lying,' he said quietly, although he had detected at least partial shock in her reaction. 'You may not have known that it was all a plot, but the idea must have occurred to you. One, you're an intelligent girl, and I have no time to waste on the seduction of your ego, I mean it. I say it only to clear the air, if we respect each other openly it will save a lot of pain.'

'All right, go on.'

'Two, your actions. I don't claim to understand the reason for all the things you've done and said, but they haven't been the good straight line that breeds trust in me. You'll have to forgive me if I allow myself some small credit for instincts. Anyway, the whole business of sending you over here with me, it was senseless even from a purely pragmatic point of view. I didn't need you to identify Zahner or to help me bargain with him. That's only a small part of it, but I know it's something you don't dare answer. No, someone at the Firm wanted you here to keep me under close surveillance, and probably to get a-hold of the file if you could and deliver it to God knows where.'

'Why have you waited this long to say it out? It seems to me you've taken unnecessary chances in trusting me this far?' Her voice had turned metallic, any artifice was gone.

Guerin paused before answering, then he did not speak until he rose from his chair and was no longer looking at her. 'Partially because I felt it was good tactics to bide my time, partially because I loved you and didn't want to get you killed. Is there anything to drink in here?'

Julia's eyes had narrowed, but she remained silent. At the mention of a drink her glance indicated half a bottle of wine left over from her dinner. He poured himself a glass, using hers, but continued to avoid looking at her. 'How much do you really know about me, Stephen? All of it?'

'All of it.' He glanced back over his shoulder. 'That everything you've told me or I've been told about you has been a lie. You're a professional. You've been with the Firm at least as long as I have. You were run into Cuba by Plans. You're caught up in the factionalism—I can guess which side.'

She sagged resignedly. 'Who told you?'

Guerin returned to sit opposite her, sipping at the wine. 'Two of our operatives picked me up yesterday. They seemed ... well informed. One of them was from Staff D.' He waited for her reaction but there was none. And yet he was certain she knew what that meant. 'I gathered he had come for you.'

'No doubt,' she said. 'They're all reactionaries in that branch, you know.'

'No, I don't know.'

'Oh, for God's sake, Stephen, drop that idiotic pose,' she

flared, 'if you want me to be honest with you.'

'I take it you're a member of the "Bourse".'

'You know goddamned well I am. You would be too, if you were anything ... but what you are.' She got up and began to pace, her fingers fluttering everywhere in an attempt to light a cigarette.

He went on. 'They planted the papers inside the Ministry of the Interior, someone they control who has penetrated the Cuban government and yet probably doesn't work for the Firm either.'

'That would seem to be it. Most of us who were resident on the island belonged to the "Bourse", the agents who came in on missions were usually the "Element".'

'Why, Julia? Why did you get mixed up in it at all?'

'Well, there's only so much I can tell you since you insist on maintaining your personal and ideological purity. Poor Stephen, the last neutral. A typical liberal.'

'I wish we had time for this sort of emotional masturbation, but we don't,' he snapped, putting the wine glass down hard on the bedside table.

She took his anger seriously. 'I'm sorry. To answer your question: those of us on the island were probably too close to the regime to hate it continuously. After all, it was part of our daily life and we could see that it was not entirely monstrous. Particularly the ones who knew what Cuba had been before. Most of the people who stayed support it, you know, and benefit from it. There is a great deal of idealism in Cuba today, Stephen, whatever you and I might think of the crimes of the past.' She hesitated. 'Maybe it's nothing more than my being black.'

He was frantically impatient to get away from the ideological and understand what he could of the only thing he could affect, the plot itself. 'Why,' he persisted, 'did they order you, especially you, to steal the file?'

Julia pondered that for a moment while Guerin shifted uneasily from the chair to the bed, and back to the chair again. 'I suppose you would have to know who "they" were. Who originally named me—I don't know. Some tiny voice in that gigantic bureaucratic anthill back there ... capriciously. Maybe a computer culled me out of the master personnel file. If it was a neutral officer—and you would have to tell me if there are any neutrals left at home —then the question is rhetorical. Fate. It wasn't one of my people, because we would have no vested interest in having a thing like this file get out into the world. Our idea if you don't know it, is to try and end this madness, not increase it. The "Element", though, might reason that the contents of the file would be doubly validated if a member of the "peace party", so to speak, were the one to bring it out. They would count on my doing my duty, in other words. Look, for all we know I may have been the only person in a position to get them out once they were placed there, it may be as simple as that.'

'Zahner?' he asked simply.

Julia scowled. They were both sliding into the unconscious symbiosis of interrogator and interrogated, where communication required fewer words and the ones that remained took on wider meaning. 'I'm not proud of that but there's nothing covert or sinister about it. Simply a gambit that failed. I wanted off the island because I had reason to believe that the struggle between the factions made me vulnerable to betrayal. The CI people on the other side sit back and wait these days. The House refused to bring me home so I applied the same sort of pressure they use on people all the time. Then, when I read the papers and realized the implications ...'

He interrupted to again point out that this was in violation of her strictest orders.

'You should have been a priest, Stephen,' she shot back.

'Is that in payment for mentioning Zahner?'

'Your naïvety is frightening. People who adhere strictly to orders are soon dead or in communist prisons. That's the way it is now. I had no intention of going to the wall or the Isle of Pines.'

'What about your future with the Firm?'

'None of us have any future. My loyalty is to the "Bourse".'

'How will they feel about you when this is over?' He got up and went to look out the window, avoiding putting himself in front of the light with practised insouciance.

She looked at the briefcase lying on the bed. 'That depends entirely upon you, I should think. Isn't that why you came back here, to tell me?'

He turned to look at her, remaining by the window. The blind was drawn but a single light down on the street crept between the slats and slanted across his face, giving it a dramatic quality he would not have liked had he been aware of it. Julia, waiting for him to answer, thought about that and was suddenly overcome with feelings of such sympathy for his innocence and lack of pretension that it constricted her throat. Guerin was momentarily disconcerted by the way she was looking at him, and it was half out of this confusion that he broke it in the way he did.

'I intend to destroy the papers, Julia.'

The smile vanished. 'No. Don't.'

'The truth is, I'd pretty much made up my mind before I came in here. But I had to know where you stood, and what would happen to you.'

'Give me the papers. We can use them, don't you see, if we have the originals, to discredit the "Element"?'

'How would you get them home? Where would you take them?'

'To people I know. There's a place in New York where I can take you. Please, Stephen ...'

He came back and stood close to her. 'We'll wait until daylight when it's safer on the streets, although I don't think you'll have to worry as long as I remain here. You can get to the embassy in Berne, the consulate here, any-

198

where you feel you've got the best chance. Go over to the other side, for all I care. As soon as you're safely clear of any responsibility I'll burn them. That's all I can do for you, Julia. I'm sorry.'

'No. It's a great deal. I recognize that.'

Guerin went back to the window. It was not nerves this time; he felt tightly but accurately under control since he had made his decision, there was no doubt in his own mind that he would be able to function until such time as he blew up his world. He had returned to the window because he had seen the Citroen of the night before parked half a block down the street.

Staring at his back, Julia asked, 'How is it you trust me, Stephen?'

'What do you mean?' He remained as he was.

'You couldn't have forgotten that you left the gun with me. And now our interests no longer converge. That combination is usually fatal for one party or the other among the people we associate with.'

He turned, smiling cynically. 'People who talk about shooting you in the back never do. Where is the gun?'

She nodded towards the night table. 'In there.'

He glanced in the general direction and then came over to her. 'I decided to trust you simply because I had to. One person. Everything else I've known is shot to hell. I think I finally know who and what you really are now, but there's no longer any way of being certain. That's why I'm going to destroy the file, my options have been reduced to one by virtue of the fact that the very idea of options has been negated. So in the end I just chose to trust you.' He laid one hand gently alongside her cheek. 'Because I love you.'

She took his hand and held it, shaking her head. 'Stephen, you're not what you think you are at all. You think of yourself as the consummate professional, but you're not that at all—you're a hopeless romantic in the most unromantic world. I'm much more of a professional than you, not because I want to be or think of it as something good—it isn't, it's shit—but because I was poor, that part of my record was accurate, and I went to Welsley and I'm dark-skinned. You were probably such a lovely boy, such a beautiful boy,' she ended up, murmuring gently.

Deeply stirred by her warmth and a softness that did not come easily, Guerin ignored the words. He placed her head against his shoulder and drew her in. 'Too bourgeois for you hard-nosed types,' he teased. 'Like Hemingway said about Henry James, something about he needed to have gone to Siberia like Dostoyevsky?'

Julia laughed quietly. 'There, do you see what I mean? That's all wrong for this time and place. You're hopeless . . .'

She broke off at a sudden pounding at the door. They were both of them stunned by the violent intrusion into the moment of private world they had unwittingly allowed themselves. A voice shouted from outside, 'Stephen, let me in—it's Sandy!' and Guerin almost reeled as he moved for the door, slammed back the lock and threw it open.

Julia cried out, 'Watch out!' but she was too late.

22

Sanford was centred in the doorway, feet slightly spread, the gun, with silencer appendaged, held discreetly at waist level, his face wearing a strained, unhappy aspect. 'Get in!' he ordered in a low voice.

'Oh, Christ!' Guerin murmured, stepping backwards in compliance. Julia, seeing the slump of his shoulders, the stricken look in his eyes when he turned to her, felt nothing but pity. Sandy stepped inside, followed by a dark man with a moustache who Julia recognized as a Captain in the Cuban G-2, Guido Cespedes. The Cuban closed and locked the door behind them.

'I'm sorry, Stephen,' said Sandy gloomily. 'Please sit down.' He bobbed the gun slightly to indicate that he wished Julia to do the same. He remained standing in the middle of the room and Cespedes leaned against the door.

Guerin continued to stare at his friend's long sad face. 'My God, I went to your family ... Helen ... the kids ...'

'I know. That was kind of you.'

'Do they know you're alive?'

Sandy hesitated. 'No, I don't think so,' he said, licking at his lower lip, 'but I hope to be able to tell them soon.' He seemed to pull himself together after that, and went over to the offensive. 'You should have listened to me, Stephen. I told you to make a choice, there were no more neutrals.'

'You weren't even honest about which side you were on.'

'That was a painful but necessary tactical evasion. You know, reversing the magnetic field. It could have been straightened out if you'd been anything less than moralistic.' He sounded proud of that part of it.

Cespedes stepped up close behind Sandy, staring at Julia over his shoulder. Softly, but loud enough for everyone to hear, he said, 'The girl recognizes me.'

'Physically,' Julia admitted, 'but I'm not sure ideologically.' Aside, she confirmed for Guerin that this was the man she had seen at the air terminal in Miami. 'Was it you put the file there for me to steal?'

The Cuban glanced at Sandy, but then nodded his head without waiting for permission, if that was needed.

'From the description I'd say you were also the assassin who went after Zahner yesterday, and blew it.' Guerin suggested.

Cespedes' face clouded but that was all the answer he

gave, although it was enough. Sandy looked on impatiently. He turned to Guerin. 'Give me those,' he said, indicating the briefcase that contained the file.

Guerin handed it over without hesitation, which surprised and disappointed Julia even though she knew there was no reasonable alternative and that stalling could only make things worse. She already had the feeling that, whatever was Guerin's fate, they intended to kill her eventually.

While Sandy went through the file, checking it, Guerin questioned him as to how he had managed the whole elaborate deception, and why.

Without looking up, Sandy explained, 'Elaborate but far from Machiavellian, I'm afraid. As you of all people might expect, Stephen, we've simply improvised around one mistake or complication after another. As usual. Hammerle isn't one of us, not with the "Element". In fact, as far as we can determine, he's one of your non-people, a neutral. Anyway, he assigned me to go with you entirely by chance. By the time we reached Manna Key it was confirmed to me that we would be bringing this young lady out along with the file. That would have ruined things for us—she can tell you why.'

Guerin looked at Julia. 'I suppose,' she said to Sandy, 'because I knew you. And you had tried to recruit me for the "Element".'

Sandy nodded as he closed the file and handed it to Cespedes. 'It was perfect from our point of view to have a person of your persuasion bring home the goods, a sort of pre-validation, but it wasn't thought worth the risk that you should see me again. Everything was going wrong by that time—you shouldn't have been on the beach in the first place.'

'I know,' Julia agreed dryly, 'that made everyone unhappy.' She turned to Guerin. 'He was the agent who brought me the order to steal the file. Only then he was called Henderson.'

Guerin was remembering that he had risked his life and gone ashore in part to protect his friend, and the bitterness of that remembrance showed on his face. He knew he was worrying petty details, but he had to ask, 'Where did you go, Sandy, how did you pull it off? Were you on the boat all the time?'

The small man's expression remained as it was, but his voice no longer betrayed pride in the circumstances as he explained them. 'It was easy enough. And my people thought it was time I went to ground anyway. I just crawled down into that stinking little engine room before we picked you up. We counted on your emotional set. Homer had shot the boat up a bit ...'

'Did a lousy job of it, too, or else he simply assumed I was even more stupid than I was.'

Sandy allowed himself a trace of a smile. 'You really did have an effect on him—he wanted to kill you. I think maybe that accounted for his sloppiness. He's dead now, by the way.' He realized from Guerin's expression what he was thinking. 'Oh, no, not us. Not even the Firm itself. He went on an assignment into the mountains of Guatemala immediately after we let you off at Manna. He was supposed to ingratiate himself with the Guerillas, but, as you saw, he lacked a lot in that respect. Anyway, the story is they found the nylon strangling cord he had tied around his waist under his clothes—you know, Special Forces stuff—and they executed him.'

Cespedes had moved to the window and now he reported that the car on the street below was flashing its lights impatiently. 'I agree with them,' he commented.

'They'll wait,' Sandy told him. To Guerin, he said a little apologetically, 'The problem with an infrastructure is it's sometimes difficult to establish clear-cut lines of command.'

Guerin almost felt sorry for him. 'You're a renegade now, Sandy.' He pointed at Cespedes, 'Like him.'

'And like you,' he was reminded. 'We know you took the file to Dr Fortin, for instance, so you won't be going home again either. At least Senor Cespedes here and myself have a kind of fraternity which we can identify with, which protects us all the way up to cabinet level. We have superiors, someone to whom we are responsible and from whom we can receive orders.' Biting off his words, he added, 'So don't waste your pity, Stephen—you always were a bit sticky and sentimental for my taste.'

'We must go,' Cespedes insisted, putting his hand on the other man's shoulder.

Sandy stood and made a show of the gun again before taking the next turn. 'I'm sorry, but she has to come with us.'

Stephen rose so quickly that Sandy had a moment of terror in which he almost shot him. The gun quivered from reflex tension and the finger on the trigger had tightened dangerously. 'Watch it!' he barked. 'I owe you something and I don't want to hurt you.' More calmly, he reminded, 'We were friends after all.'

'You can shove that kind of friendship up your ass, where it belongs.'

Cespedes stepped forward with the clear intention of searching Guerin, who remarked that it was a bit late for that if they thought it was necessary. Sandy asked Guerin if he was armed and the latter replied that he was not, actually thinking only of arms being carried on his own person at that moment. Neither of the antagonists up to now had seriously entertained the idea that life and death would become an issue. Neither had ever killed a man, although Guerin had once fired upon and wounded a Hungarian border guard while covering an escape. But that had been at a distance with a rifle and, once you were past moral considerations, there was no doubt that the mere fact of space made it simpler, easier ... thinkable.

'Why am I going with you?' Julia asked them.

Cespedes looked at Sandy, who blinked and said, 'I don't know.'

'You do know, Sandy. One of your people below is from Staff D. Why do they want her and not me?'

'I may have had something to do with that, Stephen. I told you I owed you some ... favours. But she's the enemy, after all.'

Guerin shook his head. 'You must know I can go back and denounce those papers as a fraud. I even think I can prove it.'

Sandy lowered the gun. His expression was almost compassionate. 'Nobody is going to listen to you, fortunately. Fortunately for you, because it saves your life, but they know at home you've been seeing a psychiatrist.'

'They could only know it through you.'

'Nevertheless, my advice is not to go back at all.'

Cespedes again took the initiative by placing his hand on Julia's arm.

Guerin caught it out of the corner of his eye and started. 'Please, Sandy ... don't take her!'

Julia looked at him with something like contempt. 'Oh, stop that heroic crap,' she hissed at Guerin. 'It's infantile. You know you can't do a goddamned thing to prevent them from killing me, if that's what they're going to do ...'

Sandy anxiously interjected that they had received no proof that this was what would happen. Of course everyone in the room was in the same trade and knew how foolish it would be to tell a victim that you intended to kill him when you were still faced with the problem of moving him from one place to another quietly.

'My God,' Stephen said, 'you can't want to do this ... You're a decent man, Sandy ... Your wife and kids, I mean, Jesus ... Look, screw the papers, they're not going to change the world, no matter what you think, but you can't mean to kill ...'

'Stop begging them!' Julia shouted, and the Cuban clamped his hand over her mouth.

'Shut up!' Sandy snarled, inches from her face, then he slapped her. Guerin stood by, helpless, but Julia regained her composure quickly. Cespedes relaxed his grip a little at a time, and the struggle was over. Sandy looked the most stricken of them all now, and Guerin understood that not only did he regret having struck the girl, but hated having done it in front of him. That convinced Guerin he would probably be allowed to live. Cespedes, at a signal, took Julia out of the room, and Sandy, who could not meet his friend's eyes, started to follow after them without a word.

Guerin stopped him. 'It can't be worth it, Sandy. You can't live with these people—you're no ideologue.'

Sanford regained some of his poise. 'This is what we do, Stephen. We can't let them take it away from us.' He turned away, seemingly having justified himself, and left the room with the gun held down against his side, out of sight but ready.

Guerin stood in the middle of the room for a moment, aimless, his hands flopping loosely, as though they were searching for something which had nothing to do with the rest of his body. The door had been left open and he could hear the three of them start down the back stairway. It was the last possible moment in which he could have hoped to act, and whatever it was specifically that broke him out of his paralysis of the will, it was nothing tangible or even in any way explicable. His mind was totally blank, incapable of direction, the muscles functioning not quite smoothly on automatic. Yet he rushed to the bedside table and removed the gun he had left with Julia. It had to be that he was running on the past, on the sum of what he was. Without bothering to pocket the weapon or mask it in any way, he dashed into the hallway and down the stairs in pursuit.

The hotel was a quiet place in a subdued corner of the

city, and there was no one between Guerin and the street now except a desk clerk, but an old man, half asleep. He hit the glass doors with his shoulder and it was only luck that prevented his cracking them through and alerting the people he was pursuing and perhaps crippling the arm which held the gun. There was a small terrace on the front of the hotel and steps leading to the street. Below him, almost halfway to the waiting automobile, which was pointed away from the hotel and was already geared up with lights on and motor buzzing, were the three people who had decided Guerin's life for him. The simple desperation of his decision threw him back on training and instinct; he placed one foot solidly in front of the other, bent his knees, and extended the gun at eye level, pointed down, towards the street. He even hallucinated a target on the man's back—perhaps that was all that made it possible. Sandy had put his gun back into his pocket and was carrying the briefcase with one hand, while the other hurried Julia along.

Guerin's first bullet was squeezed off evenly, without unnecessary motion, and passed through Sandy's left lung. The second divided the spleen and dropped him to his knees. No one would save him after that. Julia proved to be the consummate professional, just as she had claimed, by immediately throwing herself to the pavement. Cespedes also did the one thing that could have saved him, he ran for the car the moment he heard the familiar lethal sound, without even looking over his shoulder. If he had hesitated or grasped for the briefcase, Guerin would have killed him too, and the way he was functioning nothing could have prevented it. The shots echoed back out of the hollow streets, and then silence returned. For some reason, and only for an instant, Guerin, with the smell of sulphur still in his nostrils, glanced at the night sky. Miraculously, the gunfire had not affected its serenity in the least. Precisely as it had been when he had worshipped it through his telescope as a child.

With a frightened roar, the car had gone by the time he reached Julia and the comatose body of his friend. She regained her feet and stood looking at him as he bent over Sandy's still thrashing corpse. 'Julia, run, for God's sake,' he begged, looking up into her face. She saw that he was crying. 'That way,' he said, pointing in the opposite direction from that which the car had taken. Why had they left him alone, he suddenly wondered; probably they had reacted in the only way possible, considering their training —make no noise, avoid scenes, don't get involved, if you can't do it without embarrassing your masters, then let it go for someone who can. He had beaten them for the moment because he no longer had a master, because he had nothing to lose. Because he was free to destroy himself.

'Where?' Julia said to him quite calmly.

'I don't care! The police will be here.' Already, lights were going on, footsteps were headed in their direction, the old desk clerk had stuck his head out the door, and just as quickly jerked it back in again. It was only a matter of minutes. 'I'll take these up to the room and destroy them.' He grabbed the briefcase and stood up. She nodded solemnly, turned without saying anything and walked away without looking back. Good girl, he thought, even at the end she knows better than to listen to me, knows that it is much better to walk than to run. Good girl, Julia, he repeated to himself—a professional. And so he was himself, for he walked back into the hotel without haste and up to his room, where he methodically burned the contents of the briefcase that had ruined his career and his life. He did it with expertise.